Praise for
Sisterchicks in Wooden Shoes!

"Robin has a true heart for God, one that shines through on every page!"

—KAREN KINGSBURY, *New York Times* best-selling author

"Grab your passport and expect to be swept away on another adventure of heart and hope. Robin Gunn's writing is picturesque, like Monet—except she paints with words. It's a story I can't wait to share with my own Sisterchicks!"

—TRICIA GOYER, author of *Blue Like Play Dough*

"*Sisterchicks in Wooden Shoes!* transports readers to the land of tulips, windmills, and Corrie Ten Boom. This delightful story tickles the funny bone while tugging on the heartstrings."

—JANICE THOMPSON, author of *Gone with the Groom*

"A sweet and familiar blend of emotions weave through this story—delight in friendships, courage to face the unknown, and the passion to savor each moment. A page-turner that sings of faith, forgiveness, God's comfort, and security to overcome today's fear and confidence to face our tomorrows."

—JANET PEREZ ECKLES, international speaker and author
of *Trials of Today, Treasures for Tomorrow*

"Robin Jones Gunn once again wraps life-changing truths in a delightful story of adventure and humor that confirms that I, like

Summer in the story, can do all things through Christ and through the love and support of Sisterchicks in my life."

—KAREN O'CONNOR, best-selling author

"*Sisterchicks in Wooden Shoes!* is much more than another entertaining installment in Robin Jones Gunn's wildly popular series. It's a reminder of what a blessed gift true and lasting friendship is."

—SHARON K. SOUZA, author of *Lying on Sunday*

"*Sisterchicks in Wooden Shoes!* is a heartwarming tale of two lives woven together with the golden thread of friendship. The special bond these Sisterchicks share resonates in our souls as they bless each other in the midst of life's difficult circumstances. In the beauty of the tulip fields, the stinky cheese shop, the windmills and canals, Holland comes alive in these pages."

—VIRGINIA SMITH, author of the Sister-to-Sister Series

"*Goede nacht!* Robin Jones Gunn does it again!"

—CYNDY SALZMANN, author of *Crime & Clutter*

"I want to be a Sisterchick! Robin Jones Gunn writes about everyday women with truth, tenderness, heart, and soul. *Sisterchicks in Wooden Shoes!* reminded me of the value of friendship, honesty, history, and love while taking me on an adventure."

—RACHEL HAUCK, award-winning and best-selling author of *Love Starts with Elle*

best buddies

sisters of the heart

soul sister

friends forever

kindred spirits

sister-friends

SISTERCHICKS
in
Wooden Shoes!

girlfriends

pals for life

chum

confidante

gal pals

true blue

ally

Robin Jones Gunn

a sisterchicks® novel

SISTERCHICKS IN WOODEN SHOES!

MULTNOMAH
BOOKS

SISTERCHICKS IN WOODEN SHOES!
PUBLISHED BY MULTNOMAH BOOKS
12265 Oracle Boulevard, Suite 200
Colorado Springs, Colorado 80921

Scripture quotations and paraphrases are taken from the following: The Message by Eugene
H. Peterson. Copyright © 1993, 1994, 1995, 1996, 2000, 2001, 2002. Used by permission
of NavPress Publishing Group. All rights reserved. The Holy Bible, New International
Version®. NIV®. Copyright © 1973, 1978, 1984 by International Bible Society. Used by
permission of Zondervan Publishing House. All rights reserved. The New King James Ver-
sion®. Copyright © 1982 by Thomas Nelson Inc. Used by permission. All rights reserved.

The characters and events in this book are fictional, and any resemblance to actual persons
or events is coincidental.

ISBN 978-1-60142-009-1
ISBN 978-1-60142-239-2 (electronic)

Published in the United States by WaterBrook Multnomah, an imprint of The Doubleday
Publishing Group, a division of Random House Inc., New York.

Library of Congress Cataloging-in-Publication Data
Gunn, Robin Jones, 1955–
  Sisterchicks in wooden shoes! : a novel / Robin Jones Gunn.
     p. cm.
  ISBN 978-1-60142-009-1 — ISBN 978-1-60142-239-2 (electronic)
  1. Women travelers—Fiction. 2. Female friendship—Fiction. 3. Americans—
Netherlands—Fiction. I. Title.
  PS3557.U4866S565 2009
  813'.54—dc22

                            2008049403

Printed in the United States of America
2009—First Edition

10 9 8 7 6 5 4 3 2 1

For Ethel Herr,
my mentor and friend, who has always carried
a bit of the Netherlands in her pocket.
Thank you for inviting me to "put my feet
beneath your table" and for teaching me how to pull
a few treasures out of my pocket.

For Anne de Graaf,
for all the reasons that keep us linked soul to soul
over all the years and all the miles. You are a gift.

And for my dad,
who served in the U.S. Army in Holland during WWII.
For the rest of his life, he retained a silent tenderness
for the Dutch. I think he passed it on to me.

An armful of colorful tulips to all my hardworking friends
at Multnomah Publishers who made this series a reality
and have been true Sisterchicks from the beginning.
(Okay, so there are a few Brotherdudes
included on the team as well.)
Thanks so much. I'm grateful to all of you.

A friend loves at all times.

—PROVERBS 17:17, NIV

The Spirit of God whets our appetite
by giving us a taste of what's ahead.
He puts a little of heaven in our hearts
so that we'll never settle for less.

—2 CORINTHIANS 5:5, MSG

The world is a book, and those who do
not travel read only one page.

—Saint Augustine

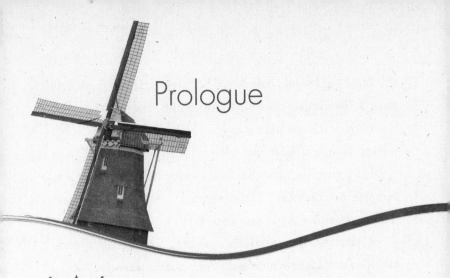

Prologue

"We do what we have to do so we can do what we want to do."

My husband has repeated that line to our children—all six of them—for the past twenty-five years. And I've viewed that as a fine approach to managing our family of eight.

But my congenial support of that philosophy abruptly ended on a stormy Tuesday afternoon last April. I answered the phone and heard one word that altered my life: "abnormal."

All of time paused and held its breath with me. I felt like a harpooned mermaid—blinking, sinking, and incapable of thinking while submerged in an ocean of fear with only the phone to hold on to as a flotation device. Outside my kitchen window the wind plucked the bright pink sprigs of new life from the apple tree and flung them carelessly across the yard.

The medical assistant on the other end of the phone said my doctor requested further tests. When did I want to schedule an appointment for a biopsy?

I told her I would have to call her back. At least I think those were the words that came out of my mouth. The only thoughts I was aware of scampering through my brain were *This can't be happening. Not like it did for my mother. Not yet. I'm not ready.*

I had spent my life doing what I had to do every day. If I was ever going to do what I wanted to do, it would have to be now. This week. Today. Right this minute.

The raindrops pelted the window, arriving on a wind-whipped wave. They came against the kitchen glass at a slant.

I wasn't adrift in the depths, nor was I sinking. Not yet. I was encapsulated. The water could press against all my windows, but it wouldn't touch me. I still was buoyant with life, and there *was* something I needed—wanted—to do.

I realize not every woman knows what she wants to do, even when given a once-in-a-lifetime opportunity to pursue her bliss. But I knew. I always had known. I wanted to go to Holland. I wanted to see Noelle.

For the past forty years, Noelle had been my closest, dearest, most supportive friend. She and I had shared our hearts with each other ever since we were paired up as pen pals in third grade. Yet we had never met face to face.

It was essential for me to steer a straight course across the vast Atlantic to the land of windmills and tulips. My lifelong dream had been to meet Noelle, and now I was going to do it before… before whatever happened next, after the biopsy.

As the spring storm kicked up outside, I logged on to the computer and scrolled through a list of flights from Cincinnati to

Amsterdam. With a brave, unwavering finger, I hit Enter. Just like that, I had an airline ticket on hold for twenty-four hours.

Staring at the computer screen, I couldn't understand why I felt such an odd sense of expectancy. I should have been terrified, but I wasn't.

Five days later I stood on Noelle's doorstep on the other side of the world, and the expectancy was still there. God was about to do a new thing. It was springing up.

I've lived at a different pace since my whirligig adventure in Holland with Noelle. I think it started with the way I floated through that stormy day last April. Somehow I believed I wasn't going to sink.

Why is it that some life-giving truths can be right in front of you but you never see them? Or maybe you do see them but don't recognize them as the solid, full-of-hope points of light they are. All that life-changing power is wasted on those of us who are oblivious, trapped in the routine of the day-to-day, forever doing what we have to do.

That's how it was for me, and that's how it was for Noelle too. She saw the truth in front of me that I couldn't see. I saw the truth she had tucked away deep inside long ago but had chosen not to see.

Both of us will say that we needed to be with each other last April more than either of us realized. We needed to look each other in the eye, open our mouths, and speak the life-giving truths that seemed so obvious to each other but not to ourselves. And in the speaking came the healing.

I do ask myself every now and then if the visit to the Netherlands truly happened or if I merely dreamed the trek. But then, to prove that Noelle and everything about her home and our deep-hearted Sisterchick friendship are real, I open my closet door, and there they are: my beautiful wooden shoes. I slip my feet into the yellow beauties, and suddenly I believe in God all over again.

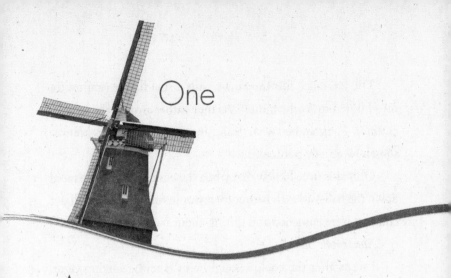

One

After booking my ticket to the Netherlands, I sat quietly in front of the computer, contemplating what to do next. Outside, the rain carried out its spring fling with gusto.

Telling my husband seemed wise. Not on the phone, though. I didn't want to say the words "abnormal mammogram," "biopsy," or "I'm leaving for a week" unless I could see his face.

So I decided to bake cookies. After padding my way to the kitchen, I pulled out a mixing bowl and turned the oven to 375 degrees.

I'm not the sort of woman who takes a long bath or a long walk to have time and space to think. For me, the best processing happens when I have my well-used mixing bowl balanced on my hip. No electric mixers for me. I beat the lumps out of my life challenges with a wooden spoon.

Then I line up all the solutions in my head while arranging the lumpy balls of dough on the cookie sheet. Soon the scent of all that lovely butter, brown sugar, and oatmeal wafts from the kitchen, and I start to feel better.

The fragrance fills the house with a standing invitation for my children to "come hither." As they gather around the kitchen counter, I remember what really matters, and my problem is somehow quietly resolved.

Only this time I knew that when the enticing fragrance raced down the hall into each bedroom, it would find no takers. All our children were launched and flitting about in their own worlds.

Abnormal. Biopsy.

I went after the cookie dough with renewed mixing vigor. Taking a few steps closer to the refrigerator, I looked over the collection of off-kilter photos until I found the one of Noelle standing in a field of tulips with a windmill in the background.

You're going there, Summer. It's going to happen. You're going to see Noelle. You really are. Believe it.

For many years a variety of photos and postcards have adorned our refrigerator. Every time I would stop mid–pot roast extraction or post–milk replenishment, the images I would look for were the ones of Noelle and her world.

How long had I dreamed of seeing those tilt-a-wheel windmills and picking those bursting-with-color tulips by the armful?

As I dropped the dough into agreeable rows and slid the cookie sheets into the oven, I made another decision. I would tell Wayne everything as soon as he came home. But I wouldn't tell anyone else about the biopsy until I had received the results. Not even Noelle.

If everything worked out for me to see Noelle, I wanted to spend my time with her as unencumbered as possible. I would take the trip in a self-induced state of denial. Yes, complete denial. It was the only way I would be able to enjoy the visit.

I foraged around in the garage for a suitcase and went hunting through Wayne's desk for my passport. The scent of warm cookies encircled me, and I thought about how one should never underestimate the power of comfort food when faced with monumental decisions. I'm convinced that the fragrance of cinnamon and sugar enlivens the heart and strengthens the senses when a woman is in want of a special measure of courage.

My courage lasted all afternoon and kept me company as I ran errands. Denial can be a wonderful thing. Why had I never called upon its fabulous powers before?

I was eager to reach home to see if Noelle had read my e-mail yet. In the rhythm of our online correspondence, I would write to her toward the close of my day, and she would read my post at the start of her new day. The time difference between our two lives was six hours. She was always six hours ahead of me. Maybe she had seen my e-mail before going to bed. Maybe she already had responded.

The rain stopped as I rounded the corner, returning home with a full tank of gas and a week's worth of groceries. Wayne's car was in the garage when I pulled in. I inched the old family minivan up to the hanging tennis ball to make sure the van was in far enough to close the garage door. As the tennis ball did its usual bounce-bounce against the windshield, anxiety surged in my stomach. Everything in me tightened. I sat in the car, waiting for the cinnamon-laced courage to come back.

I wasn't afraid of what Wayne would say. He is a great husband. I didn't always think that, but I do now. The longer we've
been married, the better our relationship has become.

The anxiety was connected to my logic in all this. How wise
was it for me to leave the country right now? What would be the
repercussions of staying in denial for another week or so?

Wayne stepped out into the garage. He peered at me through
the windshield with a half-eaten cookie in his hand. "You coming in?"

I nodded but didn't move.

"Summer?"

I couldn't quite get my body to open the door and exit the car.

"Honey, are you okay?" Wayne came over to the passenger
side. He opened the door and climbed in. His current position at
our church as one of the associate pastors includes most of the
counseling load. Wayne is a careful listener. He is intuitive and
empathetic in his approach, which was quite an adjustment from
the "Wild Wayne" I had married when I was nineteen years old.
Life, love, loss, and raising six children had had a marinating effect
on his heart. He is a big softy now.

"Is it one of the kids?" Wayne reached over and wove his fingers through my nearly shoulder-length brown hair. With a steady
hand he massaged the back of my neck. "What is it? What's wrong?"

I let out a long sigh and then exhaled all the details, starting
with the phone call and rolling right into how I had put a flight
to Amsterdam on hold and had e-mailed Noelle, asking if I could
come see her for a week.

Then I sat very still, my hands clutching the lower rim of the steering wheel, waiting for his response, which I knew could go either way. The neighbor's schnauzer barked. The car's engine pinged.

Wayne untangled his fingers from my hair and said the last thing I expected. "Good for you."

I turned to take in his full expression. "Does that mean you think I should do this? I should go to the Netherlands?"

"Summer, for as long as I've known you, you've talked about meeting Noelle. Yes, I think you should do this, and, yes, I think now is the time to go. The biopsy can wait another week or so, can't it?"

"I think so."

Wayne took my hand in his. "Do you remember what you told the kids when they left the house?"

I nodded. My farewell line was the same for each of them, and after saying it six times, I was quite familiar with the utterance. I just hadn't realized that Wayne had heard me say it. Or had remembered it.

"You told the kids, 'Go make your own adventures, and come home often to tell us about them.'" He smiled. "I'd say it's time for you to do the same. Go make your own adventure, honey. When you come home, I'll want to hear all about it."

I leaned over in the front seat of our van and kissed my husband good. Yes, I did.

The next morning I woke at four. My efficient subconscious started in immediately with a flutter of directions.

You should confirm your reservation now. Don't wait until the twenty-four hours are nearly up. The price could go up.

Wide awake, I slipped out of bed and went to the computer to check my e-mail. I wasn't going to pay for the ticket until I knew if the timing of my visit was convenient for Noelle.

Her response was waiting. The subject line of her e-mail contained one simple, perfect word: "Come!"

Over the next four days, I took care of all the necessary travel preparations, and I gave my husband more deep kisses and tender looks than he had received from me in some time.

I boarded the plane with everything I needed, including a sense of expectancy and a gentle sort of peace I had come to recognize over the years as the peace that "surpasses all understanding," which is how Scripture describes it. I love it when God grants that sort of peace, because it truly does "guard your hearts and minds through Christ Jesus."

One of the first things I did after the plane took off was to pull out a book Wayne had presented to me as a travel gift. The chunky paperback was a travel guide to the Netherlands that he had checked out from the public library. That's how tight our finances were and how ridiculous it was that I had charged this flight to Amsterdam on our credit card.

On the inside cover of the book was a map of Europe with the compact country of the Netherlands highlighted in red up in the top left side of the continent. Compared to the dominant landmass of France that curved into the equally full-bodied shape of Spain, the Netherlands appeared to be the equivalent of a ruffled peony tucked behind Europe's ear.

After the in-flight meal was served, I skimmed through the "Things to See and Do" section of the tour book. A smile came to my lips as I read one of the opening lines: "The best time to view the famed tulip fields as well as catch the final bloom of the daffodils is the middle of April."

Today was April 13. I couldn't have planned the timing better. But then, I was beginning to believe I wasn't the One who had planned all this.

I snuggled into my seat and thought about how I hadn't been anywhere internationally since Wayne and I had adopted our two oldest daughters from Korea twenty-five years ago. We had to update our passports four years ago when we attended our niece's wedding in Toronto. Aside from that, I hadn't traveled much.

I closed the tour book and closed my eyes. A lulling sleep settled on me. Sometimes when I get caught up in a novel, I fall asleep with the book in my lap, and I dream about the story. This time, when I dozed off on the plane, I floated into a dream with tour-book images of the Netherlands mixed with impressions of flying over the ocean.

I saw myself as if I were seated in a toy plane held in the hand of Almighty God. He was standing outside of planet Earth and propelling the toy airplane across the Atlantic Ocean with a soft whirring sound, as if the plane were a determined honeybee heading for the bright red peony fixed behind Europe's ear.

In my half-awake, half-asleep state, I thought of Micah, our middle son. He must have been the inspiration to my subconscious for the bee image. Micah is worried about the honeybees. He says the homing devices God built into the bees have been magnetically scrambled as a result of microwave towers around the world. Bees load up with pollen and then can't find their way back to their hives.

I sank back into the vivid dream and saw myself flitting about with Noelle inside the bright red peony, loading up sweet moments. Just as I was about to make my way back to my home "hive," I woke up. A bit of drool moistened the corner of my mouth. I dabbed it and looked around, having no idea how long I had nodded off.

I reached for my purse and pulled out a tiny bottle of eye drops. My contact lenses seemed exceptionally dry. Noelle wears contacts as well. We know an extraordinary amount about each other for never having been in daily, side-by-side life together.

Adjusting my position and tucking the blanket around my legs, I thought about how Noelle and I knew a lot of facts about each other, but we didn't know any of the details that make a person dimensional and real. For instance, I didn't know what her voice sounded like. I suppose we could have called each other over the years, but we never did. I didn't know what the back of her head and the bobbed style of her blond hair looked like. I didn't know her gait when she walked or if she kept her fingernails short or long. Did she wear perfume?

In my half-awake state, Noelle seemed for a moment to be a character in a novel I had been reading for so long that she had become real in my imagination.

But Noelle was real.

And now I was crossing not only the ocean but also the one-dimensional world in which our friendship had grown all these years. In a few hours printed words were going to be exchanged for audible words. Photographic images of each other would come alive in three dimensions, and those "images" would move, laugh, and smile.

Noelle and I were about to meet for the first time, and I felt inexplicably shy.

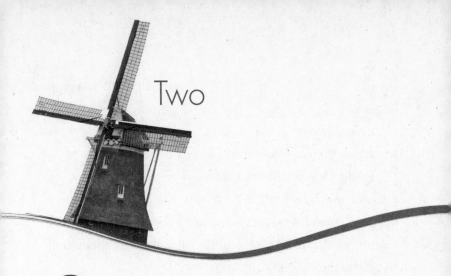

Two

Our plane slid through thick rain clouds before landing on the long, wet runway. If Noelle's world was a place of windmills and tulips, they weren't visible from the air.

I made sure I had all my belongings before exiting my seat and meandered down the long aisle to the front of the plane, where the flight attendant bade us farewell in both English and Dutch.

I followed the group through customs and on to baggage claim. Signs were posted in several languages, including English, so I had little difficulty figuring out what to do. I could see why the tour book said this was rated the best airport in Europe. Not that I had experience at any other European airport but simply because I didn't feel lost.

As soon as I retrieved my luggage, I walked toward the exit and into the open area where the general public waited for arriving passengers. I walked slowly, turning my head right and left, trying to spot Noelle. My stomach fluttered with the sort of anxious butterflies I feel whenever I'm asked to stand in front of a group to speak.

I wasn't about to stand in front of a group; I was only going to stand in front of Noelle. But still, I didn't know what to say.

Noelle's last e-mail indicated she would wait for me at the exit. But which exit? What if I should have gone in a different direction after collecting my suitcase? I already had passed the security line. I didn't think I would be allowed to turn around and go back to the baggage-claim area.

Maybe I should stand in one place and let her find me.

I stopped walking and stood to the side, hopeful that she would spot me. She would recognize me, wouldn't she? Of course she would. And I would recognize her. It was just that so many people were milling about.

Around me swirled the mixed sounds of different languages. A tall businessman on his cell phone spoke in a deep voice that echoed in the crowd. A harried mother called to her prancing child, pointing to the rest room and trotting right behind him. A young couple with pierced noses and leather jackets stopped in the middle of the traffic flow, arguing with expressive hand gestures. A young man pushed a wheelchair containing a woman who held in her lap an explosive bouquet of yellow, red, orange, and pink tulips.

Shoulders back, lips pursed in a tight smile, I looked right and left again, feeling more alone in a crowd than I had ever felt before.

What if she isn't here? What if she was delayed and couldn't get a message to me? What should I do?

I tried to think if I had a phone number for her. I'm sure I had her phone number at home, but in my scramble to pack, had I written it down anywhere? No, I was certain I hadn't scribbled it anywhere. I had no backup plan. I hadn't exchanged any dollars into euros. Should I do that now? Did the pay phones work the same as they did in the U.S.? How would I dial information? Would the operator speak English? What would I even ask the operator?

The butterflies in my stomach turned into stampeding elephants.

What if something happened, and she sent me an e-mail, but I didn't read it because I didn't check my messages before leaving for the airport? Or what if—

And then I saw her.

Tall, calm, walking toward me, looking older and more regal than I had pictured from her photos, Noelle spotted me and smiled.

I smiled back. We were like two third graders in our timid approach, each moving toward the other until we met halfway and shyly said, "Hi," at the same moment.

We gave each other an awkward hug, and I laughed. All the stomping elephants and fluttering butterflies escaped in the exhale of my laughter. The stampede must have been obvious because Noelle gave my shoulder a comforting squeeze.

"You're here." Her voice was soft, like a really great latte.

"Yes." Now my response came out short, quick, and breathy. "I'm here."

"Your flight was good?"

She was so composed. I tried to mirror her, drawing my chin up and taking a deep breath through my nose. "Yes, the flight was good."

"Good."

Noelle's navy blue peacoat was topped with a raspberry-colored scarf, which looped around her neck once and hung long down the front. Her smile was as wide as it was in all her photos. She was taller than I expected. Or maybe the thick-heeled boots she wore under her gray pants elevated her.

Despite my attempt to remain composed, I laughed again and then switched from smiling and laughing to smiling and crying.

Noelle let out a light, slightly nervous laugh. Her eyes glistened.

At the same moment we dropped all the formalities, and in a spontaneous surge, we wrapped our arms around each other again. This time we hugged as if we were sisters separated at birth who were at last reunited. On the ends of her straight, pale hair I caught the scent of sweet almonds and sugared vanilla.

In that moment I knew coming here was a good decision.

We drew back and held each other at arm's length, both staring, taking in the three-dimensional sight now that the reality of what was happening sank in.

Noelle laughed again, and I followed, my plumped-up cheeks catching the glimmers of my teary joy.

"You have such a great laugh, Summer! And I love your hair. The last picture I saw of you, your hair was so short."

I fingered the ends of my brown hair that almost touched my shoulders. "I've been growing it out for quite a while."

"Come." Noelle reached for the handle of my suitcase. "Let me take that for you. Do you need a rest room? Something to drink? It will be a bit of a ride home. Not too long because the traffic should be light this time of day, but if you would like, we can eat something here. Are you hungry?"

"I…I don't know."

Noelle smiled generously when I said I thought I had displacement shock.

"I have plenty to eat at home, and we can always stop on the way if we like. I'm afraid the weather isn't going to allow me to show off the best parts of the countryside today, but the forecast says the rain will clear tomorrow. We'll have time to see plenty during your visit. I still can't believe you're here!"

"Neither can I."

"Come."

I trotted beside Noelle, picking up my usual pace to keep up with her. She had a steady, brisk gait, the stride of a woman who knew where she was going. That was certainly consistent with how her life had played out.

We stole glances at each other, smiling in response, as if we both knew what the other was doing—gathering the visual data that had been missing all these years.

"You don't look tired at all," she said, leading the way to the car park. "Are you tired?"

"I slept a little on the plane."

"You seem so tranquil."

"Tranquil?" I was sure my e-mails of the past few days hadn't come across as anything close to tranquil. She probably expected me to arrive in a complete dither.

"I thought when you arrived, you might be more… What's the word for it? Here we say, *'Je zit niet lekker in je vel.'*"

I raised my eyebrows. I was surprised at how natural it sounded for Noelle to roll off a sentence in Dutch. "What does that mean?"

"Something like 'You're not sitting in your own skin.'"

"And what exactly does that mean?"

"Nervous. Rattled. That's a better word for what I'm trying to say. You don't seem rattled."

"I'm not. I'm still wearing the skin I left home in."

Noelle laughed. Her laugh was different than I had expected. It was light and airy, like very thin metal wind chimes when ruffled by a slight breeze. Somehow I always imagined her with a belly laugh.

"What about you? Have I rattled you too much by showing up on such short notice?"

"Yes." Noelle smiled. Her blunt reply seemed honest, but at the same time she seemed to enjoy giving me her answer the way two friends enjoy teasing each other.

"I am rattled. And I'm grateful. This is a good time for you to be here, Summer. Although, to my way of thinking, anytime would be a good time for you to be here."

"As I said in my e-mail the other day, I'm content just to be by myself when you have things to do. You don't have to entertain me. I really hope you didn't alter your schedule because of me."

"Of course I altered my schedule. For all the best reasons. You came to see me. Do you think I'm going to leave you alone in your room for one minute? Not a chance. Don't worry. All is well. We can work out the details as they come."

Noelle reached into her pocket for her keys. She stopped at the first row of cars in the parking garage and stood behind a squared-off, small blue car. It didn't resemble any model I had seen in the U.S.

"Here she is. My little Bluebell. I got an excellent parking spot, don't you think?"

"You did. What a cute car."

"Yes, she is a cutie. And small, right? All the cars here are small, but don't worry. There's room in the back for your suitcase."

I went around to the passenger side and waited while a woman in the car parked beside Noelle's opened her door and got out. She looked at me and said something in Dutch. I was caught off guard. She repeated her statement or question a little louder, as if I hadn't heard her in the cavernous garage.

"Noelle?" I called out, trying to keep my expression toward the woman friendly.

Noelle popped her head up over the top of the car, and the woman repeated her statement a third time. She sounded impatient.

Noelle responded with several sentences in Dutch. The woman said something else. Noelle nodded her head and spoke again in Dutch.

With a brusque nod to me, the woman stepped past me. I slipped into the car and looked at Noelle. "What did she say?"

"She was asking about the construction. She wanted to know

if this part of the terminal had a detour for the arrivals, because last time she was here, it was blocked off."

"Oh. She certainly seemed upset."

"Why?"

"She had such a stern expression."

"Oh, that. Dutch people don't come across smiling and flowery to strangers. It's normal to be polite but to the point. Once you get to know someone, then the smiles come."

Noelle turned the key in the ignition and glanced over at me. "Are you okay?"

"Yes. It's just…I was… It's so strange to suddenly be in a place where somebody says something to me and I have no idea what she's saying."

"Yes. Well, you don't have to be concerned about that quite so much. If you're trying to communicate with a Dutch person, and they're under sixty years old, you can speak to them in English. Usually they'll understand you and answer in English."

"Seriously?"

"Yes. Of course I'm serious. We're a very progressive nation. A lot of our television programs are in English, so that has made a difference. Especially for the children of this generation."

Noelle began to back her car out of the parking spot. From the other side of the adjacent row of parked cars came the sound of screeching tires.

"What is that?" Noelle looked over her shoulder and continued to back up.

The sound of the squealing tires intensified. I tried to look out the passenger window. In the side mirror I caught sight of a large utility truck barreling down our row, headed right for us.

Noelle shouted something in Dutch, jammed the car into Drive, and thrust her right arm out in front of me as if providing a flesh-and-bone safety bar to ease the anticipated impact.

I opened my mouth, but no sound came out.

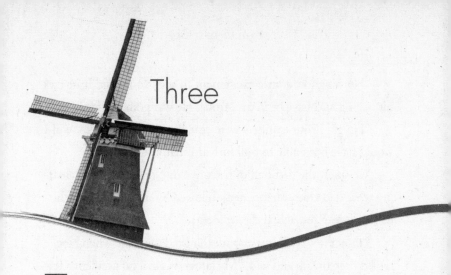

Three

The utility truck missed the back of Noelle's little Bluebell by mere inches before coming to a screeching halt when it hit a waist-high concrete barrier. Almost immediately we were confronted with the scent of burned rubber.

Noelle and I sat in a stunned sort of quiet as the driver clambered out of the truck and walked around to the front of it to examine the damage. He appeared to be uninjured.

"I can't believe he's all right," I said in a whisper.

"He must have had a problem with the brakes or some sort of engine failure." Noelle carefully shifted into reverse and eased the car out of the parking space once again.

We slowly drove past the accident site. Several individuals had gathered around, and from what we could tell, the driver really did look like he was okay. He was talking with another man, who was on his cell phone and nodding his head.

"They're calling for help," Noelle said.

"That was really close."

"Nothing like a little excitement to start your visit! If he had hit us, it could have been disastrous. He was going so fast."

"I'm glad your instincts were equally quick. I don't know if I would have been able to pull forward that fast."

We spent the first half of the drive to Noelle's home evaluating what had almost happened, followed by stories from our histories of near and actual car accidents.

I thought we had just about exhausted the topic when Noelle took a deep breath and said, "My father was in a car accident a few months ago."

"I'm so sorry to hear that. Is he okay?"

"I think so. It happened last December."

"This past December?"

She nodded.

"Noelle, I didn't know."

"I didn't write you about it. There wasn't much to say. My brother called and said Dad was in the hospital with a broken leg and some broken ribs. I know he spent a few weeks in the hospital, and then he was moved to an assisted-living center."

"And you haven't gone to see him?"

"I haven't been back to the U.S. since my mom's death. That was more than twenty-five years ago."

Noelle had grown up in a small community in Wyoming. When she and I were paired up as pen pals, her first letter to me was on stationery that had a cowboy in the bottom left corner. I still have that letter.

"I'm really sorry to hear about your dad's accident. I hope he's on the mend."

Noelle looked straight ahead and kept driving. "You know that he and I…we haven't had much of a relationship ever since… well, since I left home."

I knew that she had made an abrupt decision to leave home right after graduating from high school, taking all the money she had been saving for college and instead going to Europe for the summer. She traveled around until she ran out of money and then took the first job she could find, which was providentially in Rotterdam, where she met her husband, Jelle.

"Your father never quite accepted that you stayed here, did he?"

Noelle glanced over at me. "Is that what I told you?"

"I'm not sure what you told me, to be honest. I just assumed your parents didn't approve of your staying in Europe instead of returning home."

"I couldn't go home."

I waited for Noelle to explain her stunted sentence. We drove in silence through steady rain. I didn't know her on-the-spot, in-the-moment personality well enough to decide whether her comment was an invitation for me to probe further or, more likely, was her closing the door on the subject.

One thing was clear. Even though I knew a lot about Noelle and the two of us had shared a lot about our experiences over the decades, parts of her life were a mystery to me. Her relationship with her father was one of them. Somehow this significant disconnect with her father never had been mentioned in our written chats.

Noelle had told me quite a bit about her mother after she passed away. And when my mother died almost nine years ago, Noelle had lots of encouraging and helpful things to say to me.

Our fathers, however, never had been a big topic between us.

"Would you like a coffee?" Noelle asked. "I could use one. We drink a lot of coffee here. Did I tell you that already? This would be a good time to stop for coffee."

"Fine with me."

The first stretch of the drive from the airport had been the familiar sort of highway that circles any large city and its suburbs. I had a vague sense of the buildings looking different and the shape of the trucks being narrower than trucks in the U.S. But in general I was more caught up in the conversation with Noelle than I was with the view out the window.

She circled a traffic roundabout, and we soon entered a residential area. I was surprised to see how narrow the homes were and how close they were built to each other. Every one of the brick houses had a large window that faced the street, and each home was separated from the pavement by a low fence with a gate that led to a small patio, which was little more than six feet by six feet. Most of the homes had flowers percolating over the rims of clay pots or windowsill boxes. Through many of the front windows I could see either a bouquet of flowers or a lamp.

I wasn't trying to take an impromptu survey of what all these homes had in their windows, but because we were driving so close to them, it was easy to peek inside. And every home had its curtains open.

"Is this typical?" I asked Noelle.

"Is what typical? The traffic? I was thinking it wasn't too busy right now."

"No, I meant the houses. They're so close together."

"Land is at a premium here. We build up, not out. Most homes are several stories. Usually three. The Dutch are very efficient."

We did a loop, circling another roundabout, and headed down a stretch that was suddenly agricultural with a marshy field where some sort of green crop was at the five-inches-high stage. I looked for a windmill but didn't see any across the flat expanse. The road we were cruising down was built up like a long, flat mound. To the side, down the mound, was a canal that ran parallel to the elevated road.

"There's your first canal sighting," Noelle said. "You'll see them everywhere. We're about to go down my favorite part of the drive home. The place I want to take you for coffee is just a little ways from here."

Noelle drove on, and I watched a smile rise on her face when she turned a corner. "This is it. This stretch with the trees lining the road. Isn't it lovely? I have no idea how old these trees are, but look at them. They're so big and shady. Each of them has a distinct personality. My girls used to call me *gek*, crazy, because I would talk to the trees as we drove this way. Now they tell me that when they drive down this stretch, they say hello to the trees."

I admired the big, burly trunks of the expansive trees and took in their branches that effortlessly sprouted thousands of new leaves. They stood like brave soldiers, wearing their scars and their prolific assortment of green medals with pride and honor.

"I almost feel as if I should salute them," I said as we sped past the end of the tree formation.

"Yes. That's it, isn't it? I never thought of it that way before, but that's what I feel too. Those trees have stood strong through sleet, snow, and hail. They remain steady in the summers, which sometimes can turn sweltering. And they keep on standing, brave and true. I feel grateful for the determined person who planted them so long ago."

We entered an area that looked like a picturesque European village from a travel brochure. The close-together shops looked clean and fresh, in spite of the obvious age of some of the taller buildings at the end of the block. The line of shops on the right side of the street reminded me of an area not far from where I live—an area that had gone through a successful urban renewal when some of the older, more charming buildings were renovated. We drove slowly down the street, looking for a place to park. As we passed a flower shop, I noticed the store next door had a large sign in the shape of a wooden shoe hanging out front.

"Does that store really sell wooden shoes?"

Noelle looked over her shoulder. "Yes. We can go in, and you can try on a pair, if you want."

I laughed. "They really sell wooden shoes here?"

"Of course. Many people still wear them on the farms. The fishermen wear them."

"Why?"

Noelle smiled. "They keep your feet warm and dry, and they don't slip."

"Do you have a pair of wooden shoes?"

"Yes, of course. For the garden. When the girls were little, they both had pink ones they wore when they went out to the family farm to see the horses."

"I thought wooden shoes were part of the Old World Dutch tradition. I never would have guessed they still make and sell them. Except maybe for tourists."

"I'm sure they sell lots of them to tourists in the larger cities. But if you want an authentic pair for a lower price, you should buy them here."

"I don't know where I would wear them."

"In the garden, of course. Especially in the spring when it's wet and rainy. They're comfortable. Really."

When I still didn't look convinced, Noelle said, "You will try on a pair before you leave. I just decided that for you. Oh, wonderful! That car is pulling out. This is a good spot."

Noelle pulled into a very tight parking place in front of what looked like a post office.

"I can't believe how compact everything is. I never could have managed to park in a spot this small. You amaze me, Noelle."

She turned off the engine and reached over to put her hand on my shoulder. "Summer, I think quite a few things about this country will amaze you. I know I've already said it, but I'm really glad you've come."

"I'm glad too. I do have one request, though."

"What's that?"

"Warn me ahead of time about any of the things you think might surprise me so I won't say or do anything to embarrass you."

"Don't worry about embarrassing me. Trust me, I have managed to embarrass myself plenty over the years. You are my guest. It is my honor to have you here. So, are you ready for a coffee now?"

"Sure. Just tell me how to ask for coffee in Dutch."

"That's easy. *Koffie.*"

"Now how do I order a grande, two-percent, half-pump, sugar-free vanilla latte with no whip?"

Noelle stopped in front of the car and stared at me a moment, apparently trying to see the joke in what I had just said. "What was all that?"

"That's my usual," I explained.

"Your usual what?"

"Coffee."

She still looked confused. "Why would you have to go through a whole speech like that just to get a coffee? What did you say again?"

I repeated my standing order, and this time she laughed.

"What is the two percent?"

"That's the milk. You can order nonfat, two percent, whole, or half-and-half. If you want your latte with half-and-half, you order a breve. Or you can order soy milk. You can have whipped cream on top or add your own chocolate powder, cinnamon, or liquid sugar."

She looked at me as if I were making all this up.

"It's true. It helps if you memorize what you want before you get to the register so you can say it all in the right order."

"What if all you want is a simple cup of coffee?"

"Then you have to ask for 'drip.'"

"It's an entire coffee subculture, isn't it?" Noelle said. "We have those fancy coffee chains here, but I rarely go to them. The last time I did, I was with my girls, and they did the ordering for me. Sounds like that was a good thing. I would have been lost on my own. Ordering will be much simpler here."

We stepped into a warm, small space that had the feel of a bakery because of the limited yet tempting assortment of treats inside the display case. An older couple sitting at the table in the corner stared at us. I glanced at them a second time and got the feeling they weren't staring in a creepy way but rather in a bored way, as if we were the best entertainment available on a dull afternoon. Why sit home and watch television when you can walk to the local minicafé, sip coffee, and watch people?

Noelle greeted the woman in the white smock behind the counter and ordered for us.

"Would you like to share a *gebak*, or would you like your own?" Noelle pointed to what looked like a flat apple tart on a plate inside the display case.

"I could eat a whole piece. It looks good."

"It is *goot*," the woman behind the counter said in stiff English.

"I'm sure it is. Tank you."

I meant to say "thank you," but hearing her *goot* instead of *good* prompted me to respond with "tank you."

Noelle gave me a quick glance as if to be sure I wasn't making fun of the woman's accent. I wasn't, but my face warmed, and I quickly stepped to the side while Noelle paid.

The people in the corner still were watching us. I hoped I wouldn't do anything to cause a scene. At the same time, I felt as if I should do a little tap dance or finger-puppet show before sitting down.

Opting to ignore the couple, I sat with my back to them. Noelle placed a small ceramic cup of dark, steaming coffee in front of me. The apple gebak was served on a plate with a fork balanced on the side. I took one bite of the dense fruit pastry and made an *mmm* sound.

"*Lekker?*" Noelle asked.

"Is that what it's called? Lekker? Is that Dutch for 'cake'?"

"No, *lekker* is the word for 'delicious.' If it's really good, you go like this." She opened her hand and put her flat palm to the side of her thick, blond hair. "You say, 'Lekker,' and then you do this." She waved her hand slightly as if fluffing up her hairdo.

"What does that mean?"

"That you like it. It tastes delicious."

"But why are you waving to your ear?"

Noelle grinned. "That is what it looks like, isn't it? I hadn't thought of it that way before. I have no idea why we do it or what it means, but if you like something that's tasty, that's what the Dutch do."

I gave it a try, waving my open palm in front of my ear. Noelle nodded her approval. "My first lesson in Dutch nuances. Keep them coming." I took a small sip of the hot coffee and swallowed it quickly. The strong taste prompted me to cough.

"Are you okay?"

"I hate to admit this, but I think I've turned into a coffee snob. Not even a coffee snob. I'm a latte snob. This tastes really strong to me."

"Oh, right! The five-percent milk."

"Two percent."

"I'll get some milk for you." Noelle went to the counter and returned with a small pitcher.

As I lightened up my coffee, I said, "I hadn't realized it until now, but I barely recognize the real stuff anymore."

"It's all right. You don't have to change over to the Dutch way of doing things simply because you arrived an hour ago." She winked. "We'll give you a week."

I laughed. "A week is all I have."

My statement stuck in my throat as soon as I said it. It was as if I had spoken a self-fulfilling prophecy. After this week I didn't know what kind of life or schedule I would have. Would I be able to drink coffee if the doctor put me on a restricted diet?

Noelle confidently lifted her chin. "Don't worry. A week is all I need. I told you. The Dutch are very efficient."

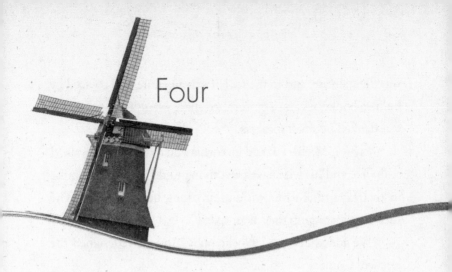

Four

Noelle's home felt familiar from the moment we drove up to it. Much of what met my eye was as I had imagined. I had seen photos over the years, with the inside and outside of the house as the background.

Many of the same distinctives I had noticed about the other Dutch homes appeared in Noelle's as well. Even though her house was only thirty-five years old, the flat front of the house led straight up to a pointed roof like the traditional houses we had seen on our drive. The front entry was a patio of pavers with flowers and a small tree, all growing in deep Mediterranean blue garden pots.

"We gave up trying to bother with grass out here," Noelle said. "This part of the house rarely sees sunlight. I've had good success, though, with a few shade-loving plants. In the summer it's nice and cool out here."

We entered, and I realized how efficiently the small space was used. Four steps in, and we were standing by a stylish black leather couch that framed the seating area in the living room. To the right was the staircase, and to the far left was an entire wall covered by built-in bookcases and a customized space where a flat-screen TV was flanked by small speakers.

"My son Michael would love what you did with that wall," I said. "He and his wife have been trying to do something similar in their apartment but without anything being built in. The shelves are eating up their floor space."

"We added all that," Noelle said. "And we redesigned the kitchen. Come."

I let go of my luggage and followed her a few steps past the couch where the room made a T. On the left was a round dining room table with a bouquet of red tulips fully in bloom. To the right was a modern-looking but very small kitchen with all stainless-steel appliances.

"It's just the right size for us now," Noelle said. "All the years while the girls were growing up, it was so small. You could barely have two people in the kitchen at one time."

I couldn't imagine the kitchen any smaller. Even with the modern upgrades, the built-in appliances appeared narrower than what we have in the U.S.

"It's impressive," I said truthfully. The space looked well used, and the shine from the stainless steel reflected cleanly the focused, canned, overhead lights. The kitchen looked as if it could be an advertisement in a magazine.

"Are you ready to see your room? It's on the second floor. We converted the attic into a third floor, and that became our bedroom. I'll show you that too."

The three stories were traversed by a set of stairs. I had seen this sort of metal, spiraling stairs in movies or in pictures but never in a home. There was no railing. Only the series of narrow metal plates that were open to the front to accommodate feet that were too long to fit on just the step. Feet like mine. Although, when I took the fifth or sixth step, I realized only a child's small feet would fit on such small stair plates.

Noelle was carrying my suitcase, which was a good thing. I'm afraid I would have had a terrible time trying to navigate the narrow steps, the spiral direction we were heading, and a bulky suitcase. Noelle hoisted it ahead of her with little difficulty. She seemed much stronger than I was. But then, if I lived in a three-story house instead of a one-story bungalow, I might have developed some impressive strength from all the hauling up and down.

After one complete spiral turn of the metal stairs, we were on the second floor. A square area anchored four closed doors. Noelle opened the one at the opposite end.

"This is the bathroom. I put clean towels on your bed. I'll be sure to give you some instructions before you run the water in the tub or shower. It's different than what you're used to, but I don't think you'll be too confused."

Turning to the closed door on my left, Noelle opened up the guest room—my room. A twin bed with a beautiful, puffy white down comforter waited for me with folded towels at the foot.

"I put hangers in the closet, but let me know if you need more. This room doesn't have a lot of closet space since we use it for overflow." She put my suitcase next to the closet. "I'll show you the office across the hall, and then we can go up to see the bedroom on the third floor."

I kept up with Noelle as she scooted across the hall and opened the door to a crowded home office. The desk sat in front of the window that looked out to the back of their house. A high-back office chair faced the window.

Just then the chair turned, and Noelle's husband lifted his hand to greet us but didn't change his facial expression.

"I didn't realize you were home," Noelle said in a soft voice.

The large, fair-skinned man nodded in a reserved manner.

Whether he was reserved Dutch or not, I was thrilled to meet Noelle's husband after all these years. I jumped in, stepping close and offering my hand in an eager handshake. "Jelly, I am so glad to finally meet you. Thank you for agreeing to let me come last minute like this."

A deep voice suddenly spoke from the speakerphone on the desk. I hadn't realized a phone call was in progress. The man on the speakerphone replied in Dutch. While I couldn't understand what he said, I distinctly heard him repeat Noelle's husband's name, "Jelly," with a humorous inflection.

I turned to Noelle with my lips pressed together just as a second voice chimed in, also in Dutch. We had interrupted a conference call.

Noelle said something in Dutch and motioned for me to follow her out of the office. She quickly ushered me out of the room and closed the door behind us. Her face was red.

I grimaced as soon as we were on the other side of the closed door. "I'm so sorry. I didn't realize he was on a conference call."

"He was talking with his brothers."

"Oh."

"They all work together and…"

I tried to read Noelle's expression. Not only did I have the disadvantage of not being familiar with what her different expressions meant, but I also didn't know if this was the sort of thing we would all brush off and laugh about later. Her husband's response had been so reserved.

"Come." She motioned for us to climb the spiral stairs to the top floor.

I hoped this meant it was best to just set aside my intrusion on the conference call and go on as if it was no big deal.

We stepped into a beautifully decorated loft with a large bed, thick rugs, and a wide window facing the outside world at the back of their home. I immediately went to the window. Gazing past the neighbors' roofs, I said, "Is that the North Sea you can catch a glimpse of between the rooftops?"

"It's Rotterdam Harbor. We can watch the huge ships come in." Noelle took my arm. "Summer, you know how you asked me to tip you off before you do anything embarrassing?"

"Yes. Too late, right? I'm sorry I barged in. I should have waited until Jelly said something to me first."

Noelle looked like she might burst out laughing.

"What is it?"

"My husband's name is Jelle." The way she pronounced it, the name sounded like *Yella*, not *Jelly*.

I slapped my hand over my mouth.

"You had no way of knowing. All these years you've only read his name. I never told you the *j* is pronounced like a soft *y*."

"Oh no! And I called him Jelly in front of his brothers!"

Noelle pressed her lips together, suppressing a giggle. "He's been called worse than 'Jelly' but…just don't ever add 'Belly' to the end of it. That would be the worst."

"Oh, Noelle! I'm so embarrassed."

"Don't worry. Really. All is well. You broke the ice. The rest of your visit can only go up from here."

I hoped she was right. We went downstairs to the living room, and at Noelle's suggestion I called Wayne to let him know I had arrived safely.

"I would like to say hello to him before you hang up," Noelle said from the kitchen.

I handed her the phone, and she graciously introduced herself to my husband and thanked him for encouraging me to, at long last, make this trek. "We have only one complaint so far," Noelle said. I thought she was going to tell Wayne how I had slaughtered her husband's name.

"Our complaint is that Summer did not bring you with her. Next time both of you must come. We would love to have you as our guests. Sincerely. Anytime."

My heart warmed to Noelle and her hospitality all over again. I had packed for this trip so sure that this was a one-and-only life-time adventure. My vision didn't include even an inkling of a "next time." I liked that she had presented the possibility to Wayne. He would know that I was keeping to what I had told him the night before I left.

That last night at home, as I was placing my cosmetics bag into a padded corner of the suitcase, Wayne came into the bedroom and stood behind me. He cleared his throat as if he were about to launch into a private therapy session. Knowing how my husband's counseling mind works and how the reality of my spontaneous decision had finally caught up with him, I was certain he had processed down to the last detail the psychological reasoning for what I was doing. He was about to offer me a diagnosis and possibly a course of treatment. His initial encouragement to "go have an adventure" was no longer at the forefront of his thoughts on this trip.

Before he could impart his wisdom to me, I took his hand. "I have a pretty good idea what you're thinking right now, but before you dive in and give me some helpful insights, I want to say this." Now I was the one clearing my throat. "Wayne, if I am about to enter a stretch of loss in my life and if denial is one of the first stages of grief, then what I would like to do is go to Holland in denial. Complete denial. I want to be all the way there. I don't want to have one foot here and one foot there. Does that make sense?"

He gave a nod.

"Whether what I'm saying is healthy or unhealthy, can you just let me do that? Be in denial for a week?"

I could almost see the gears grinding to a halt in Wayne's head. He adjusted his glasses and did this thing with his jaw, as if he had been hiding a piece of gum in there and now would be a good time to soften it up again. The man literally chews on his words before he speaks them. I have come to be grateful for that trait; it means he's being deliberate.

Wayne's response was, "Okay. I'm here for you."

I smiled. My heart immediately felt lighter. The "I'm here for you" line was one I had asked Wayne to use early in our marriage. After three miscarriages and then the challenging process we went through to adopt our two older girls, I had heard every bit of resourceful wisdom from everyone. Including—and especially— from Wayne.

When I miraculously did conceive at last, the dear man tried every tactic he could to cheer me and bolster my strength during the difficult pregnancy and long delivery. His endless advice got to be too much for my exhausted body and brain. At last I told him, while at the hospital in the midst of the birthing process, "The only thing I can handle hearing from you right now is, 'I'm here for you.' That's it. No advice. No motivation techniques. Just be here. That's all I ask."

In the same way he was just there for me at the hospital so many years ago, he was once again there for me the night I packed for this trip.

When Noelle handed the phone back to me, I said "good-bye" and "I love you" to Wayne. In appreciation for his support of my choice to stay in denial, I added, "Thank you for being such a wonderful husband. I'll be home in a week."

His closing comment was, "I'll be here for you."

I handed the disconnected phone back to Noelle.

"You're smiling. Did he say something sweet to you?"

My nod was my only answer.

"He has such a soothing voice. I think I would want to go to him for counseling just to hear him say in his calming voice that everything was going to be okay.

"Now." Noelle turned her attention to the items she had lined up on the kitchen counter's limited space. "We were thinking we would make fish tonight with some vegetables and potatoes. How does that sound? Any allergies or food preferences I should know about?"

"No. What can I do to help?"

"You can go up to your room, unpack, and relax a little. I'll call you when dinner is ready. Jelle and I want to make this meal for you. This is what we do. We cook together. In our small kitchen it's a well-orchestrated event."

"So, basically you're telling me I would be in the way down here."

"That's exactly what I'm telling you."

"Okay, I'll go upstairs. Call me if you change your mind and I can do something simple like set the table."

"Thank you but no. I have all of it taken care of."

I climbed the stairs, ducking my head as we both had done earlier to navigate the spiral passageway without stumbling or bumping our heads. After entering the guest room, I closed the door behind me and suddenly felt weighted down. It was as if the gravity in this corner of the world were stronger than it had been when I first arrived. Was this what jet lag felt like?

It was early in the afternoon at home, but somehow I had missed a night's sleep as I had jetted through the time zones. Of course I should be tired by now. A short rest was immensely appealing.

Kicking off my shoes, I stretched out on the bed. One minute on that luxurious, thick comforter and I was transported to the place where dreams are vivid. I could see floating tulips on the insides of my closed eyelids. Red tulips, like the bouquet on the dining room table downstairs. Red tulips and small ceramic cups with coffee so dark that when the stream of milk was added, it formed a swirling white design on top.

I have no idea how long it took Noelle to awaken me with her persistent taps on the door. I stumbled to open the door, trying to grasp a memory, any memory, of where I was. When I looked at her, blurry-eyed and blinking, the fragrance of baked fish and roasted potatoes brought the connecting pieces together more quickly than Noelle's face.

"I hate to wake you. It will help you adjust to the time if you come eat before going to bed. Really, it will. Are you hungry? Come."

"I'll be down in just a minute."

I couldn't remember the last time I had felt so fragmented in mind and body. If my dream on the flight was coming true—if God had picked me up like a toy airplane and directed me like an eager honeybee, and if He had hand-sailed me to this bright peony that adorned the north-turned ear of Europe—then I could very possibly be suffering from having collected too much pollen on my first dive into the bounty.

I was weighted down and felt as if I could barely move.

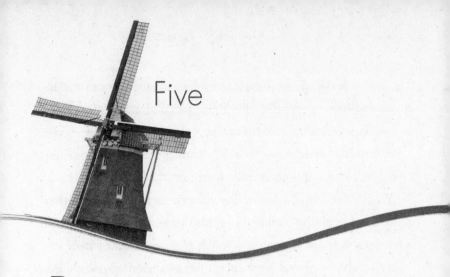

Five

Blessedly, the heavy-handed sensation from the jet lag lifted, and what followed that evening was extraordinary. Jelle and Noelle's hospitality at dinner that first night was beyond anything I had experienced, including all the holidays I had spent with my large and loving extended family.

Jelle and Noelle didn't serve over-the-top food, although all of it was very good. What escalated their hospitality was the calmness and kindness that accompanied the meal. I was invited to enter into a relaxed and lingering conversation. Their serenity and acceptance transformed what could have been a very simple meal into a time of fellowship and celebration. They were celebrating me—my visit.

Considering the mental and physical state I was in when Noelle woke me before dinner, I bounced back rather quickly. Before going downstairs to join them, I splashed my face with cool water, brushed my hair, and returned to the guest room to change into a fresh blouse.

I took the stairs carefully and found the living room dotted with a dozen lit votive candles along with a grouping of various-sized candles arranged in the center of the glass coffee table. Classical music played softly. A plate of triangular-shaped crackers, topped with a shrimp spread, waited on the coffee table. Each cracker was adorned with a tiny sprig of some sort of herb that looked like a tiny feather and transformed the appetizers into miniature works of art. Next to the plate were three small cut-crystal glasses. Several beverage options awaited us in tall, chilled bottles.

"This is beautiful, Noelle. Thank you for going to all this trouble."

Noelle had changed into a freshly pressed blouse as well, making me glad I had taken the time to do the same.

"It's a treat, not a trouble."

Jelle offered me the plate of appetizers. Evidently he had brushed off my faux pas earlier in his upstairs office. If he wasn't going to bring it up, neither would I.

He and Noelle sat back on the couch, and I settled comfortably into the matching leather chair that faced them. In hushed voices we entered into a lilting conversation.

So this is the purpose of appetizers. They aren't merely for keeping the kids out of the kitchen when I'm preparing the meal.

Jelle asked about my children and husband and said, "Please greet them for me."

"I will."

At his gentle questioning I ended up telling how we came to take in two foster children. After adopting our two daughters, I unexpectedly carried two babies—a daughter and then a son—to full term. Content and blessed with our four children, we weren't looking for more. But then we met Micah, and Micah had an older brother.

"We didn't want the brothers to end up in different homes, so we became foster parents for Micah and Derrick, who was nine at the time."

I kept going with a few more details of our unusual, combined family. Our life sounded out of the ordinary when I described it, but all the years I had been in the middle of just living it, it seemed normal to me.

"I thought our home was full with two daughters," Jelle said. "You had three daughters and three sons. I honestly cannot imagine."

"I loved it. Well, most of the time. We had a lot of noisy, crazy, busy years, but Wayne and I both came from large families and wanted a large family. This may sound old-fashioned, but my life goal was to be a wife and a mother. A good wife and a good mother."

Jelle tilted his head. "This is not a goal one hears so much these days. Although, good wives and mothers do receive congratulations. In the Netherlands, when someone has a birthday, it is for the family members that the congratulations are given."

I looked to Noelle for an explanation.

"It's true. On my birthday, if you lived here and you saw Jelle, you would shake his hand and say, 'Congratulations on your wife's birthday.' "

"I've never heard of anyone doing that before," I said.

"That's what we do," Jelle said.

Noelle nodded. "A few years after I moved here, one of Jelle's sisters gave me a sign in Dutch that said, 'Don't try to understand. It's Dutch.' The sign had a double meaning, of course, because I was trying to learn Dutch, and there was much I didn't understand. But it also was meant as a reminder that even if I didn't understand one of the family traditions, I should go along as if it made perfect sense. His family members still shake their heads at me and some of my deeply rooted American ways."

Jelle raised his glass and offered a toast. "Congratulations to your husband for your accomplishing your goal to be a good wife and mother. A good mother."

Taking my cue from Noelle, I went along with the toast and tipped back the last of the juice I had selected from one of the chilled bottles. "This is so good. What kind of juice is it?"

"It's a blend of several fruits. Highly concentrated. It's healthy. I'm not sure I know all the names in English anymore. I know it has blueberry, and is it lingonberry? Do you have that berry in the States? It's popular in Scandinavia. Anyway, it's my favorite appetizer juice. All you need is a few sips to wake up your appetite. Speaking of appetite, are you interested in having some dinner now?"

"Sounds good. It smells wonderful."

Noelle invited us to gather at the dining room table, which she had set with dark red place mats, shiny black dinner plates, and thick-handled flatware. The vase of red tulips was encircled by votive candles in small gold cups that cast an alluring glow across the table.

The setting was so beautiful and the serenity of the moment so peace giving, I felt as if I could slowly enjoy this meal with my tender-hearted friends and then go back to the airport and board a plane. I would fly home rich in what I had hoped to gain from this trip—all in less than eight hours.

However, as I was discovering on this journey, God had much more to give to me. The elegant candlelit dinner with Jelle and Noelle was only the beginning.

I couldn't recall a time when I had felt so celebrated. I also couldn't think of a time when I had initiated or participated in a gathering that expressed so much honor and so much unrushed simplicity. No matter how much effort I had put into preparations for a birthday or holiday meal, I couldn't remember a party when we were undistracted. Someone would have to leave early. Someone was in a bad mood. The phone rang. The time together never flowed as effortlessly as it did at Noelle's home.

I didn't know how much of that was inspired by Dutch tradition and how much was Noelle's temperament and the daily rhythm of grace she danced to with Jelle.

Time seemed to curve to their bidding. Nothing in the world was more important than our leisurely time together and their careful attention to the details. I felt honored, which is the best gift one friend can give to another.

Crawling into the guest bed after dinner and sinking into a deep sleep under the thick comforter, I was certain I would sleep around the clock and not wake until at least ten the next morning.

My prediction was wrong. I woke before dawn. After my efforts to fall back to sleep failed, I reached up to lift the window shade to peek outside, and the shade stayed in the partially open position.

Lying back down, I tried to convince myself this was the time to sleep. *Sleep, sleep, sleep. Come on! Sleep!*

My efforts were in vain. Sleep had left the building. I was alone in the darkness except for a faint tinge of rose that laced the predawn clouds outside the window.

I noticed a book on the small table next to the bed and picked it up. It was a devotional. In English. After I bolstered up the pillows behind my back, I opened to a page entitled "Unfolding Grace." At the top was a portion of a poem by John Greenleaf Whittier.

Drop Thy still dews of quietness,
Till all our strivings cease;
Take from our souls the strain and stress,
And let our ordered lives confess
The beauty of Thy peace.

I paused before reading further. What I had experienced at dinner only hours earlier was a living demonstration of those words. Peace.

The next portion of the entry on that page was from 2 Corinthians 4. "So we're not giving up. How could we! Even though on the outside it often looks like things are falling apart on us, on the inside, where God is making new life, not a day goes by without his unfolding grace.... The things we see now are here today, gone tomorrow. But the things we can't see now will last forever."

I leaned back, lowered the book into my lap, and gazed out the window. The morning sky definitely was blushing now. It was as if God had invited the shy new day to come and spread her beauty over this corner of His world, and she was being obedient but at the same time was embarrassed to be put in the spotlight of the rising sun.

I wondered how many viewers of the dawn were in her audience this morning as I was, there in my sheltered perch. This quiet moment felt like a rare privilege, seeing what I was seeing.

It seemed a good time to pray. I thanked God for bringing me safely to Noelle's home. I thanked Him for orchestrating this crazy, last-minute adventure and blessing me with such a great start with my longstanding pen pal.

I looked out the window again and thought I should ask God for something. But what? Had I ever asked Him for anything for myself? I had spent most of my life praying for others. For my husband, for our children. I had asked for finances, wisdom, direction, and lots of health needs on behalf of others. What if I asked God for healing?

What came to mind was the biblical account of Hezekiah, one of the kings of Judah. As he lay dying, languishing on his bed, he turned his face to the wall and prayed that God would spare his life. God healed him and gave him fifteen more years.

Should I ask God for fifteen more years?

Suddenly I realized I had jumped from the denial stage of grief to the bargaining-with-God phase.

Stick with denial. That's where you want to stay this week. You can jump around to the anger and bargaining after you get home.

For now, just enjoy this trip. Look how Noelle is going all out to make this a wonderful visit. Don't ruin it, Summer.

I read the Whittier quote again, taking in the first line: "Drop Thy still dews of quietness, till all our strivings cease…"

I wanted my striving to cease.

Then turning my face to the wall, or, more accurately, the window, I watched the day slowly inch her way to center stage as the curtains of darkness were drawn back. I felt the quietness that filled the room. I took small sips of the "unfolding grace" of the coming dawn.

And I didn't ask God for anything.

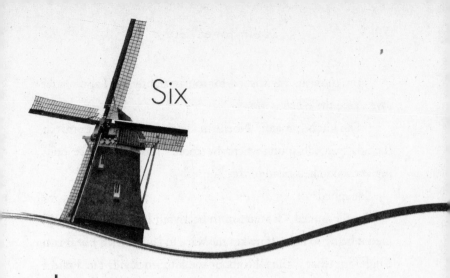

Six

"Jelle suggested we make a list," Noelle said as she unloaded the dishwasher later that morning.

"A list of what?" I sprinkled a spoonful of granola over a bowl of strawberry yogurt.

"A list of things to do and see while you're here."

In spite of my having been an early-morning audience to the new day, I somehow had managed to float back to sleep while I was propped up in bed and had slept until almost nine o'clock.

Noelle rinsed out her coffee mug and placed it in the dishwasher. "I told him we might enjoy our time together more if we didn't have a schedule."

"Either way is fine with me. I don't have anything specific in mind. Well, actually, that's not true. I do want to see a few things, if it's convenient."

"Let me guess. You want to see a windmill. And a field of tulips, of course. I've already thought of the best place to go to see those."

"Yes, those are my wished-for tourist sights. But I also would love to see the *Kitchen Maid*."

"The kitchen maid?" Noelle made a sweep with her arms in the tidy space all around where she stood. "That's me! You're looking at the kitchen maid of this house."

I laughed.

Noelle smiled. "It is so fun to hear your laugh. I never imagined it being so light. It makes me want to laugh when I hear you laugh. So, what is the joke about the kitchen maid? I'm afraid I don't get it."

"I was referring to the painting by Vermeer. You saw the original painting at a museum when you first came to Amsterdam and sent me a postcard of it."

"I did?"

It surprised me that Noelle didn't remember.

"Yes, it's a beautiful painting. I kept the postcard on my refrigerator for years and years. It got so crumpled I finally put it away in the box where I've kept lots of your letters."

Noelle looked at me with an expression of amazement. "You're kidding. You still have the postcard I sent you way back then?"

I nodded.

"I don't remember what postcard I sent you, but I do remember sending one. At the time I was afraid you wouldn't want to be pen pals anymore once you found out I had flown the coop, so to speak."

"Of course I still wanted to be pen pals. You only made it more exciting to correspond because your letters and postcards now came from the other side of the world."

"Yes, but do you remember when we were in high school and we had that whole string of letters planning our big move to New York?" Noelle asked. "We were going to be roommates and start careers in modeling."

"You were the one who was going to pursue modeling. I wasn't sure what I was going to do, aside from find a job and marry someone who was fabulously wealthy."

"Right. I remember the fabulously wealthy plan. We both were aiming for millionaires, weren't we?"

"I remember rehearsing how I was going to explain to my parents why our plan to move to New York was a good idea. None of my practice attempts were very convincing. So in a way I'm glad you stayed here. I never had to make my pitch to my parents."

"Glad that worked out for you, then." Noelle had a wry grin. Her blond hair was tucked behind both her ears, and with her fresh morning face, she looked young. Younger than I felt at the moment.

"Did your parents ever understand your choice to marry Jelle and stay here?"

Almost immediately Noelle's expression changed, as did her posture. "No." Her grin vanished. "They didn't approve or understand." With her chin up she said, "Enough of the past. We have some living to do today. You want to go to the Rijksmuseum, then. We can do that. Today, if you like."

"Is that where the Vermeer painting is on display?"

"Yes. I think a number of his paintings are. The museum is in Amsterdam. I haven't been there in a long time, but I can look up the information easily enough. Do you like Rembrandt? Many of his works are there as well."

I felt a little unexpected flutter. "Rembrandt? Really?"

With a grin over her shoulder, Noelle said, "He was Dutch, you know. Van Gogh, as well. We'll definitely go to the Van Gogh Museum in Amsterdam. I can check on times. Should we go today? Or would you rather see the tulips first?"

The sudden realization that I would have a chance to see original artwork by greats like Van Gogh, Rembrandt, and Vermeer caught me off balance. "Yes!" I said, not having paid attention to her question.

"Which one? Tulips or Amsterdam?"

"Either. I don't know. What's the weather supposed to be like?"

"Cool. Partly cloudy."

I hesitated, not sure what to suggest.

"Was anything else on your list to see?" Noelle asked. "The town of Gouda is kind of fun for tourists. They play up the interest that visitors have in the cheese, of course, so you might enjoy that."

"A cheese tour wasn't on the top of my list. Now, if you want to take me on a tour of a Dutch chocolate factory, I wouldn't mind. Especially if they give out free samples. To be honest, I don't want to run around trying to take in a whole bunch of tourist spots. I would love to go to the museums in Amsterdam and to the tulip fields, and if it's convenient, I would like to go to Haarlem."

Noelle gave me a surprised look. "Haarlem? Really? Why there?"

"I'd like to see the Hiding Place."

"What is the Hiding Place?"

"It's the watch shop and house where Corrie ten Boom lived and where her family hid the Jews during World War II. Have you ever been there?"

"No, I haven't heard of her."

Now I was the one with the look of surprise. "You haven't heard of Corrie ten Boom? She was Dutch. She and her family were sent to a concentration camp for aiding the Jews. Many of her family members died there, but she was released and spent the rest of her life traveling around the world talking about her experiences as well as writing books."

Noelle shrugged. "We hear a lot of stories about the war here. Everyone still remembers. It affected that entire generation in a way that…" She drew in a deep breath. "How do I explain this? It's not like we have war celebrities here, you know? Too often it turns out that the people who brag about having family who were heroes during the war actually are covering up something. The ones who really did fight the Nazis hardly ever talk about it."

"That's interesting because in the U.S. we have a strong tendency to go looking for people we can lift up as heroes. Wayne says we put anyone on television who has something to brag about."

"Here it's not like that. A true Dutchman will give and show kindness in quiet ways. He doesn't want anyone to know about his heroic or generous acts. I think it goes back to the Calvinist roots and the verses in Matthew that say when you give, do it in secret. Don't let your right hand know what your left hand is doing."

"Doesn't it then say that God, who sees you in secret, will reward you?"

Noelle nodded. "That's very much a part of the culture here. You know, if you want to see a World War II museum while you're here, the Anne Frank Museum is interesting. That's also in Amsterdam. We could go there, if you like. I don't know if it's similar to the house you're talking about in Haarlem, but it's extremely moving."

Just then the phone rang. Instead of the ring I was used to at home, Noelle's phone had a dull buzzing sort of ring. Instead of a brief "hello," Noelle answered by giving a short greeting in Dutch. I was pretty sure she inserted her name into the greeting.

I looked out the window and saw that the clouds were beginning to clear. A few feet away, on the other side of the backyard fence, Noelle's neighbor stood on a ladder, trimming a tree. He made eye contact with me but didn't wave.

I looked away and carried my dishes into the kitchen. From where I stood by the sink, a bush with bright purple blossoms blocked part of the view out the window. I realized it also blocked the neighbor's view into that portion of the kitchen.

Our home wasn't large, but our back lot and front yard combined would encompass the entire compact block where Noelle's home was situated with five other houses. We never considered our home and yard to be very big or especially valuable compared to the newer homes that went in up the road. Some of those houses had tennis courts and swimming pools. Our yard contained some nice trees and a lot of grass that needed to be cut all too often this time of year.

Having space to look out on an uninterrupted view felt normal. I didn't know how I would feel having to live with common walls where two families were carrying out their lives on either side of my home, only inches away through the dry wall and insulation. The hushed tone of the dinner and soft music from last evening made more sense.

Noelle hung up from her call and joined me in the kitchen. "So, what did you decide? Tulip fields today?"

"Sure. We could go to the tulip fields. The weather looks like it's clearing."

"Good. I need to make a quick phone call. I'll be ready to go in about ten minutes. Be sure to bring a coat in case the weather turns on us."

I went upstairs and gathered what I needed for the day. When I returned to the living room, Noelle was on the phone, speaking in Dutch and smiling. She hung up and gave me a big grin.

"What are you smiling about?"

"I have a surprise for you."

"You do? What is it?"

Noelle laughed. "It wouldn't be much of a surprise if I told you, now would it? I have a little treat for you tomorrow. There, that is all I'm going to tell you. No more hints. Today we'll go see the tulips."

"And a windmill," I reminded her.

"And a windmill." Noelle linked her arm with mine and led me to the front door. With a smug grin she said, "Today will be good, but tomorrow will be fantastic."

"You're a brat, you know."

"Me, a brat?" She laughed. "I haven't heard that word in ages. I can't believe you just called me a brat!"

"Well, what would you call it in Dutch if your friend had a secret surprise and took great delight in taunting you with it? Surely you have a comparable term."

Noelle thought only a moment before popping out the Dutch word, "'*Oen.*' And you're right, Summer. I'm being an oen. And I'm loving it!"

"Oen," I spouted as we exited the front door, our arms still linked. A neighbor getting into her car turned and stared at me.

Noelle unlinked our arms, looked away, and pressed her lips together as she unlocked Bluebell. As soon as we were inside her car, she burst out laughing. "I can't believe one of the first Dutch words I taught you is *oen*, and that's what my neighbor heard you call me!"

"Is it a bad word?"

"Not really. Not here. It might be considered rude in the U.S. I don't know anymore."

"Are you saying that *oen* is more derogatory than the term *brat*?"

"I would guess so. Yes, a little."

"Great!"

Noelle laughed delightedly. "Let me see. What other questionably rude words can I teach you?"

"Don't even think about it. I'm withdrawing my enrollment from your school of Dutch lessons. Obviously you're only safe when we're both speaking English."

"I know some German." She glanced at me sideways as she backed up the car.

"Not interested."

"A little French perhaps?"

"No thank you."

"You're spoiling all my fun." Noelle put on an exaggerated pout. "You just wait until tomorrow. That will be fun."

"It will be more fun if you tell me what we're going to do."

"All right, fine. Since you're so insistent, tomorrow we are going to…" Noelle continued her sentence with a long trail of Dutch words and a coy grin from ear to ear.

I shook my head at her. "Not fair."

"Yes, well, if you had stayed in Dutch school and worked on a few nouns here and there, you might have been able to pick up enough to figure out what we're doing tomorrow."

"I'll willingly settle for being a dropout and remaining in suspense for the next twenty-four hours, especially since my ignorance seems to bring you such glee."

Noelle reached over and squeezed my arm. "Having you here is what brings me glee."

I felt the same way, but I didn't say anything. I was too busy taking my turn at being a brat. Or should I say, oen, whatever that meant.

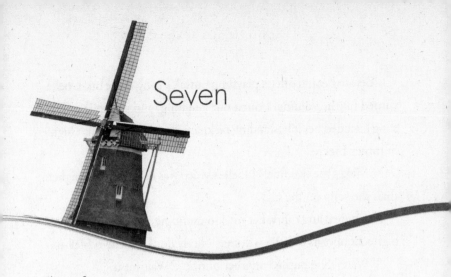

Seven

Noelle drove about a mile with the playful expression still clinging to her lips. Suddenly she blurted out, "I almost forgot! I have another surprise for you."

I rolled my eyes in an exaggerated attempt to look put out. "And exactly how long are you going to make me wait for this surprise?"

"You don't have to wait. I'm going to give it to you now." She reached forward and pressed a button. "Ready?"

"My surprise is that your car has air conditioning?"

"No, wait for it. You certainly are impatient in person, you *oenie*!"

"'Oenie'? What is that?" It sounded as if Noelle was saying "moonie" without the *m*. Before Noelle could answer, I caught myself and said, "No, don't answer that. You're tricking me. I'm a Dutch language school dropout, remember?"

"I'm going to answer you anyway. An oenie is my own softened version of an oen."

Before I could offer a playful rebuttal, a song came on. Noelle turned up the volume. I burst out laughing, and so did she. The song included her longstanding nickname for me since junior high: Summer Breeze.

"Makes me feel fine!" Noelle's voice was off pitch and higher than the song on the CD.

I laughed and called her my longstanding nickname from our high school years of letter writing. "Nicely done, Noelle-o Mell-o."

"Wait!" She pushed another button. "Wait for it."

The tune that had inspired her nickname came on in all its "quite right" funk, and both of us broke into a fit of giggles.

"I burned this CD for us. Do you like it?"

"Love it! Can you make a copy for me?"

"Sure. At least I think I can. This was my first attempt. My daughters do this sort of thing all the time. I'm just figuring out the technology. Wait. You have to hear the next song."

Noelle pushed a button and nothing came on. We kept driving and listening, but no happy sounds came from the CD player. Noelle pressed another button and turned up the volume until right in the middle of the song, John Denver's voice filled the car with a Rocky Mountain high that nearly blew out our eardrums.

We laughed, and Noelle quickly tried to adjust the sound. She pushed the Start button again, and a Rocky-Mountain-high note that seemed capable of rattling the windows blasted us. The volume seemed ineffective with John Denver's vocals, so Noelle turned off the CD, mumbling, "Okay, so my technology skills are a little questionable."

"However, your choices for travel music were superb, Noelle-o Mell-o."

"Thanks for trying to put a nice coat of varnish on my mess." Noelle pulled back into the flow of traffic and didn't try the CD again. She said it was too dangerous when we were on the road.

While we were still rosy from the afterglow of the gigglefest, Noelle said, "Not only are you the sole woman in the world who can get away with calling me an oen in front of my neighbor, but you are also the lone woman in the world who has ever called me Noelle-o Mell-o!"

"Really? Noelle-o Mell-o is such a great nickname."

"That may be true for you and me, but believe me, you are the only one who can call me that. And until this moment, that nickname had only appeared in writing in your letters. I still have the letter where you drew the picture of what was supposed to be me with a very mellow expression."

"You do? I remember drawing that picture. I was in my room listening to my brand-new transistor radio. Remember those? I was stretched out on my bed writing the letter to you, and that song came on. I drew the little sketch and wrote 'Noelle-o Mell-o.' "

"Quite right," Noelle echoed in a low voice.

I chuckled. "Crazy, isn't it, the random moments in life you can remember decades later?"

"I'm simply glad your inspiration was that particular song. I shudder to think what my nickname might have been if you heard something else on the radio at that moment. Something like... 'Rocky Raccoon' or 'Yellow Submarine' or..."

"'La Bamba,'" I offered.

We laughed again, both smiling and settling into the comfort of being together.

"You can call me Noelle-o Mell-o all you want. I don't think anyone else in my life would ever call me that because I'm not known for my mellowness."

"I'm surprised by that. I did picture you as more…"

"Quiet?"

"*Subdued* might be a better word."

"Try *repressed.*" Noelle shook her head slightly. "At least that's the word I would use to describe myself while I was under my parents' roof."

"Was your childhood pretty awful?" I kept finding myself caught off guard whenever Noelle mentioned her parents or childhood with a bitter edge.

Noelle shifted in her seat and made a right turn before answering. "I'm sure my childhood was much better than most people's."

"Your letters never hinted at a lot of angst." I was still fishing for details. But I didn't know if I had the right bait on my line of thought or if I would be able to haul in the truth if she did bite.

After a thoughtful moment Noelle said, "I think whenever I wrote to you over the years it was always a downshifting time for me. I would stop all the running around, breathe deeply, and take inventory. I'm sure a lot of my letters were like American Christmas letters. We still get a few of those every year. They are always a tidy, upbeat summary of the highlights for that family, along with a photo of everyone smiling. I think for a while most of my letters to you were like that."

"Not all of them. You and I both have opened up a lot to each other over the years. I know I've written things to you that I wasn't ready to talk about with anyone else."

"It's been the same for me. Especially in my early married years. I think I've always wanted to give you a good impression of me, but at the same time I needed to open up my heart to another woman who understood what I was feeling. Especially an American woman. Does that make sense?"

"Yes, it makes a lot of sense. I felt that sisterly sort of sharing in our letters. I always have. Our correspondence over the years has probably been better for us than we realized."

"You mean as an outlet?"

"I was thinking more along the lines of therapy."

Noelle chuckled. We were heading down a long stretch of flat road with rows of houses on either side.

"You wrote such fun letters, Summer. I saved almost all of them in a big cookie tin. Someone gave my mom a big tin of shortbread cookies for Christmas one year, and I loved the red plaid on the side of the tin. When I went back to Wyoming for my mom's funeral, I found the cookie tin in the attic, and I brought it back with me."

"I remember your writing an e-mail and telling me that."

"I did tell you, didn't I? You know, sometimes, especially since everything is done so quickly now with e-mail, I forget what I write. I compose e-mails in my head, and then I'm never sure if I sent them. Do you do that?"

"All the time. I don't think I forgot that often with letters. Maybe it has something to do with the tactile act of touching the paper and holding a pen. I don't know, but I agree with you. I'm forever telling my kids that they never answered my e-mails, and they say, 'What e-mail?'"

"I don't know how you keep it all straight with six kids. I don't know how you did it when they were all at home and in school. I have great admiration for you, Summer. Here I was, giving a round of applause to Wayne; you deserve the praise as well."

"I feel as if all you've done since I arrived is affirm me. Thanks, Noelle."

"It could be I'm trying to make up for a few times when I slipped up in being supportive in our friendship over the years."

"What do you mean?"

"I never told you this, but I felt guilty when I wrote to tell you I was expecting Tara. You had been trying so hard to have children and had gone through those terrible miscarriages, and here we weren't even trying, and we were pregnant. I think I was five months along before I finally wrote you."

"I was happy for you. I really was."

"I know you were. You were so sweet about sending gifts for both the girls. I did a horrible job of remembering your children's birthdays and—"

"Hey, don't do that. Don't compare. I never felt slighted by you. You expressed genuine interest and love for all our children every time you asked about them. That meant just as much to me as if you had sent cards to them on their birthdays. We show our love in different ways. That's okay."

Noelle glanced at me. "You're right. It is okay, isn't it?"

I smiled back. "Yes, it is."

The ease of our give-and-take conversation felt as natural as if we had spent many hours together like this, side by side, over the years. Even though I had fluffed up the notion early that morning that I could have gone home before breakfast and felt satisfied with the visit, I was glad I was still here.

I knew in my heart that if I opened up to Noelle about the biopsy and my encroaching fears, she would lovingly process all my thoughts with me. But I didn't want to process them. I wanted to push them back into the basement of my emotions and simply live. I wanted to celebrate and enjoy life the way we had last night at dinner. I was determined to gather as many rich and meaningful experiences as I could this week. I planned to save them in the scrapbook of my memory so I could return to view them fondly in the days ahead. I would look at this time with Noelle and say to myself, *Well, at least once in my life I did something I wanted to do.*

Noelle turned the car into the large parking area at the tulip gardens. The lot was filled with cars as well as tour buses. We weren't the only ones who had decided to visit the tulips that morning, and I soon saw why.

The attention to detail in the opening to the park was breathtaking, with a path leading us into a garden area with blossom-filled trees. Carefully laid-out groupings of brilliant yellow daffodils were circled by stalwart grape hyacinth. Bunches of red tulips stood together like a squirming elementary school choir ready to break into song as soon as the first note of spring was struck. A sea of thick green grass surrounded all the flowers and trees.

I stopped and pulled out my camera.

"What are you doing?"

"Taking pictures."

"Already? This is only the entrance," Noelle said, "not the flower fields."

"But it's so beautiful."

She looked around at what I was admiring. Behind her flowed a steady stream of visitors moving on toward whatever it was that lay past the end of this carefully designed path.

"You're right. It is beautiful. Do you want me to take a picture of you with the tulips in the background?"

"No, I just want the tulips." I snapped shots and was grateful we had entered the digital age. I would have gone broke on all the rolls of film I would have needed to snap pictures to my heart's content.

"Here, stand right where you are. Look this way." She had pulled out her camera and was taking a picture of me anyway. With her face still behind the camera, she said, "This is so I will keep my promise."

"What promise?"

"I promised that one day, when you came to the Netherlands, I would take your picture so your smile could end up on someone's refrigerator. Do you remember?"

I smiled broadly. Yes, I remembered. And so did she. That was what made our friendship golden.

"Come." Noelle motioned for me to join her in the flow of people moving toward whatever tributary lay at the end of this garden path. We stayed on the walkway, taking our time to view the meticulously groomed flower beds that lined the lane. Photo ops were presented to us at every turn.

At the end of the trail, we came into an open view of a flat field alive with color. Rows of flawless bright tulips filled the space as if they were a lake reflecting a sunset with ribbons of red, yellow, pink, orange, and white. All the rows were perfectly lined up. The eager-to-please tulips stretched toward the powder blue sky, strong and brave on their vivid pogo-stick stems.

I never had seen anything like it. I never had felt such speechless appreciation for something as simple as flowers. I wanted to cry but had no tears. Only a tightening in my throat.

"What do you think?" Noelle took off her sunglasses and looked at me as if trying to read my expression.

"It's...beautiful."

"Wait until you see them up close. Come." Noelle led the way with her camera in hand.

The tulips grew in mounds of rich, dark earth. Between the straight rows of tulip mounds were well-trampled "gutters" in which visitors were permitted to walk through the muddied earth to get up close and personal with the upturned beauties. Hundreds of visitors strolled up and down the designated narrow pathways between the blooms. The groupings of people seemed to bob along in the lake of beauty like sailboats and rowboats set adrift on a calm day.

The first row we traversed bore white tulips. I stopped to stare. At a distance they looked like simple ivory tulips. Up close the delicate flowers became more intricate. They had what looked like ruffles along the top edges. Inside the cuplike petals were faint streaks of pale pink you wouldn't notice unless you stared straight down into them to discover their hidden beauty.

"Unbelievable," I said under my breath.

Noelle snapped a picture of me bending close to examine the details of a white ruffle-edged tulip. I'm sure my expression when I looked up was one of childlike awe. I felt like a child experiencing one of the simple wonders of the world for the first time. I had seen tulips, but never had I imagined a tulip like this, with such intricacies.

And that was only my first tulip.

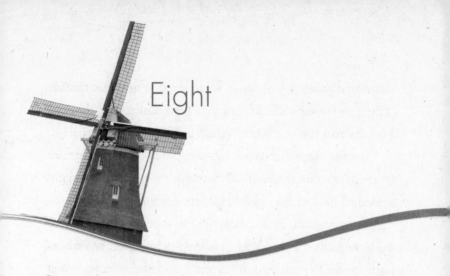

Eight

I looked up from the singularly amazing ruffled bloom that had so captured my attention and once again felt the sense of being afloat on a lake of tulips. Such vivid colors! The sunlight highlighted the blooms so all the colors were sharply focused. For one heart-tugging, breathtaking moment, I closed my eyes. It seemed impossible to take in so much glory all at once.

With a broad, sweeping gesture, a cool breeze brushed past us and moved through the tulips like an invisible hand rustling them from an enchanted sleep.

"Look!" My voice was just above a whisper. "They're dancing!"

Noelle grinned and made soft agreeing sounds. "It's beautiful, isn't it? I love coming here. Do you want to walk around now and see some more? My favorite ones are over this way. Come."

I followed her the way a child wades into the water, feeling safe because a protective hand is within reach. In my mind's eye I wasn't envisioning Noelle's hand being in reach; I was picturing God's. Surely His hand was the invisible one that had just brushed over the sleepy heads of the tulips and sent shivers down their stems and mine. I wondered if He loved seeing His children delight in the sight of such beauty. Did moments like this thrill Him the way they thrilled His children?

"I came here last week," Noelle said, breaking into my moment of contemplation. "I brought a woman who recently started coming to our church. Her family doesn't yet know that she's attending church, but she never had toured the tulip fields in the seven years she's lived here. I offered to bring her, and when I went to pick her up, her mother and grandmother came as well. Her grandmother especially loved the tulip fields. Even though it rained, we still trekked up and down all the rows."

"I see now why you said that wooden shoes come in handy here."

"Yes. Now you see. This is a good place for wooden shoes. I should have brought mine last week. Today it's not so muddy."

As we talked, we strolled past a lovely lineup of petite yellow tulips. We were nearing the center of the field, making our way to Noelle's favorites—the deep red ones—when she said, "Look up."

I drew my fixed gaze from the endless line of tulips and glanced back to the parking area. There, far to the left, was a sight that had been hidden from our view by a dense grove of trees.

"A windmill!"

"There you go. Your first windmill. We only have a few hundred left in the country that still work. I don't think that's a working one."

"Not to sound like a foreigner or anything, but what do windmills do exactly? I mean, I'm guessing they are a source of energy—"

"Nonpolluting, natural energy," Noelle interjected.

"Yes, but for what? Grinding grain or something?"

"Yes. When thousands of windmills were here in the low-lands, the wind, of course, turned the sails and ground the grain. But they still are being used to distribute water and drain the polders. We have lots of water issues here, you know. Lots of canals. At Kinderdijk near Rotterdam, if we go up there, I'll show you some windmills that still are working to keep the floodwaters back."

"So it wasn't the little boy who stuck his finger in the dike that saved Holland from the ocean? It was really the windmills that saved the day?"

"I have no doubt the legend of the little boy contains some truth, but, yes, the real heroes are windmills," Noelle said. "Much of the Netherlands is below sea level."

"Like New Orleans."

"Yes. And we all saw what happened there when the waters weren't held back."

"I never realized the Netherlands was so vulnerable."

Noelle bent down and cupped her hand under a bloom in the first patch of deep red tulips we came upon. Her motion was similar to the way a loving mother would cup a child's chin and look into sweet eyes with unconditional approval.

"Yes, vulnerable. Aren't we all? And yet somehow we remain protected by God."

I nodded, feeling vulnerable there in the midst of all the fragile beauty. Vulnerable and yet protected by God.

Am I protected really? God obviously allows devastation in His

*world and in His people. What about with me? What is He doing
with my body? What is He going to allow?*

I shook off the disturbing thoughts and looked closely at the
tulips in front of me.

But apparently Noelle's thoughts hadn't floated away from the
tulips as mine had. "This is where I bought the bouquet I have on
the table at home. They sell bouquets at the gift shop. You might
have noticed that picking the tulips isn't allowed."

I felt a primal urge to stealthily pluck just one, simply because
Noelle told me I couldn't. "There are so many. Why don't they let
people pick what they want and then charge them by the quan-
tity on their way out?"

"Because if you pick them at this stage, the bulb comes up
with them. You have to cut them. Besides, the tulips here aren't
grown for bouquets. Almost all the tulips in the Netherlands are
grown and harvested for their bulbs. The bouquets are not the big
commodity; the bulbs are. They are exported around the world."

She leaned down to gently stroke the soft petals of an exceptionally large red tulip as if it were an endangered species and
needed tender care to keep producing.

I lifted my camera to catch the shot.

She adjusted her position so the bevy of beauties framed her
face. The sunlight seemed to ignite her blond hair, causing her to
look as if she were wearing a halo. The contrast between the red
tulips and her golden hair was stunning.

"You look like a little Dutch girl. All you need is one of those
hats with the wide wings that stretch out the side and curl up at
the end. Like the flying nun's hat. Remember that TV show?"

Noelle laughed. "Yes. Here the traditional costumes are called *klederdrachten*. You only see elderly people wearing them at special festivals. They're hard to find. It's kind of like going to San Francisco and trying to find a bonnet."

"Well, you look like a darling little Dutch girl just the way you are, you and all those little red-hot-mama tulips."

"I think I would rather be described as a red-hot mama than a darling little Dutch girl."

"As you wish, red-hot mama. Now go ahead and pose for me all you want. I'll keep taking pictures." I lined up another shot.

"Here. Take one of me tickling the tulips. That's what my girls used to call it when we came here. They would go up and down all the rows and touch the flowers like...what was that game we used to play? The one where you tap people on the head, and then one of them gets up and runs after you?"

"Duck, Duck, Goose?"

"That's the one! My girls had a game like that. They played Duck, Duck, Goose with the tulips."

"Only I'm guessing the tulips never got up and chased after them."

"Well, one time..." Noelle broke into an engaging grin just as I snapped the shot. "I'm only kidding."

"Keep on kidding. It's making for some great expressions in these shots."

I kept clicking away as if I knew what I was doing, which I didn't. We switched places, and Noelle got me to smile and laugh with the red-hot mamas while she took pictures.

We continued our self-guided tour for over an hour. She took pictures of me, and I took pictures of her, and then we took pictures of our taking pictures of each other.

The laughter flowed. Some of the shots I took were up close while others were taken from the start of a row of tulips. I was interested in trying to capture the uniformity and precision of the rows, the heights of the flowers, and the symmetry of the opening blooms.

Hundreds of other visitors around us were doing the same. Never had I heard so many different languages at one time. Yet everyone, from every culture and language, seemed to have some sort of equivalent to "Smile" or "Say cheese" right before taking a shot. I wondered what they were saying.

The visitors also seemed to all say the equivalent of "Beautiful!" or "Amazing!" in their own languages. In a way this field had been transformed into an open-air cathedral, and Creator God was being praised in dozens of languages by hundreds of souls in awe of His handiwork.

"Did you know that tulips originally came from Turkey?" Noelle asked.

"Seriously?"

She nodded. "They aren't indigenous to the Netherlands, but everyone thinks they are because the Dutch turned them into an export industry more than four hundred years ago."

"I'm still amazed at how straight all the rows are."

"That's Dutch precision for you."

"This morning I read from the devotional book you left by my bed. The prayer for today had a last line with something about 'let our ordered lives demonstrate Your beauty and peace.' I don't remember the words exactly, but I was thinking of that while looking up and down all these rows. An ordered row or an ordered life really does demonstrate beauty and peace, doesn't it?"

"My father-in-law would like what you just said. He has a farm." Noelle bent down to look closer at a wide-open pink tulip. The flower seemed to snuggle to her touch the way a dog relaxes when scratched behind the ears. "When I first came here, I couldn't believe how hard my father-in-law worked and how detailed he was about everything he did. He was the king of orderly rows of crops and an orderly routine to his life. He was successful in a very quiet, unnoticed way and well respected for his criticism."

"Did you say for his criticism?"

"Yes. His critical comments were highly valued. Individuals took what he said about them or their work with great appreciation. Sounds odd, doesn't it? This was one of the most difficult parts of the culture for me to adjust to because I'm so big on praise and affirmation. I'm still not sure I fully understand it."

"Are you saying that a critical comment is more highly valued than a compliment?"

"Something like that. Here, when a person hands out praise and compliments left and right, he is considered a flatterer and insincere. More than that, he is seen as… What's the term? Simpleminded?"

"An airhead?"

"An airhead." Noelle laughed. "I hadn't heard that term

before. That's good. That's what a person who compliments a lot would be considered. On the other hand, a person who offers constructive criticism is considered caring and smart. That individual tells it like it is, which reflects more thought and intelligence."

"I would have a hard time adjusting to that way of thinking."

"I did at first. Now I have settled into a sort of hybrid of Dutch thought and American ways. I still hand out far too many compliments and praises, according to my husband, although I have had some influence on him. You saw how complimentary he was of you at dinner last night."

I nodded.

"I'm also still too loud and expressive to be mistaken for a true, hundred percent Dutch woman. Jelle says you can take the girl out of the USA, but you can't take the USA out of the girl."

"I don't see that as a bad thing."

"Neither do I." With a sly grin Noelle added, "This is one of the reasons your visit is so good for me. It gives me a chance to be my good ol' US of A self around someone who understands."

"You can be as US of A around me as you want." We were heading toward the gift shop, so I added, "If by any chance they carry American flags in the gift shop, I'll buy one for you."

Noelle laughed. "I doubt you'll find any. But if we find some wooden shoes, I will buy those for you."

We entered the gift shop and found wooden shoes, all right. Every size and color. We found key rings with tiny wooden shoes dangling from the end, wooden-shoe planters for flowers, and wooden-shoe Christmas ornaments.

The swarm of visitors had increased in number and nationality, it seemed, since we first had arrived. The gift shop felt unbearably crowded.

Noelle selected a big bouquet of mixed colored tulips and was standing in line at the checkout. I opted for buying an ornament for my Christmas tree.

Noelle insisted on purchasing the ornament along with a second one she had picked out for me. My selection was a hand-painted, cutout ornament of a red tulip. Noelle's choice for me was a pair of yellow wooden shoes dangling from a long black ribbon.

"They look like ballet slippers hanging from their satin laces." I held them up and watched the wooden shoes sway like wind chimes.

"Well, you saw how the breeze made the tulips dance. You can just consider wooden shoes to be the Dutch dancing shoes, if you want to go sway with the tulips."

I loved both of the winsome reminders of our fun day together. More than likely I wouldn't tuck the ornaments away and wait until Christmas to hang them on the tree. I would find a special place at home, like the swing arm of the lamp behind the couch or the corner of my bathroom mirror. That's where I would hang the little hand-painted charmers.

Every time I looked at them I would remember this morning—the morning Noelle and I went bobbing on a lake of dancing tulips. If I ever doubted that any of this spectacular day really happened, I would have hundreds of pictures as evidence, red-hot mamas and all.

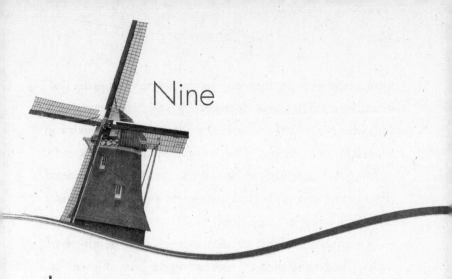

Nine

Leisurely taking the road back to Noelle's, we stopped for lunch at a restaurant that Noelle said was known for its omelets. We chose a table outside under a wide, orange-striped umbrella. I settled in and noted that overhead the unhurried clouds floated like enormous, abstract sheep grazing in a field of faded blue, freshly mown "grass."

Noelle and I talked about a thousand small nothings. Both of us commented on how fun it was to talk about everyday girlfriend topics such as which vitamin supplements we were taking, why we found it hard to stay motivated to exercise, and what sort of dental floss worked best—waxed or unwaxed. From there we easily slipped into bemoaning the advance of our underarm wobbles.

We were having fun just talking and not having to run a spell check on words like *cellulite* or *elliptical trainer* before sending off our comments. Here, the sentences were simply going across the table, not across the e-mail expanse.

We ordered dessert, of course. Then we laughed. We had just

spent a solid forty minutes decrying the injustice of sagging bodies and agreeing that the only recourse was to try harder and stick with whatever weight-loss or health-improvement methods had worked for us in the past. Then we ordered some sort of creamy pudding that came with whipped cream on top. But we ordered only one and split it. That had to count for something in terms of our efforts to stay in shape, right?

I wasn't bothered that we talked so much about health-related topics. The conversation fell more along the lines of beautification than life-altering health issues such as I might soon be facing. For now, at the outdoor café under the orange-striped umbrella with the fluffy lamb-clouds frolicking overhead, I felt healthy, alive, and interested in picking up a few tips on combating under-eye puffiness.

Noelle leaned back in the middle of a statement she was making about the virtues of cotton undergarments compared to nylon or silk and said, "I just heard myself. Are we talking about underwear?"

I laughed. "Yes. Are you embarrassed all of a sudden?"

"No, I'm used to having these sorts of conversations with my two daughters, but I think I got carried away having you to talk to. We should be talking about something else."

"What else should we talk about? Politics? No thank you. Our children? That's all we talked about at dinner last night. The way I see it, we have a lot of years to catch up on all these girlfriend topics. We've spent years preparing short summaries of our lives and giving reports to each other in our letters. If we want to talk about things like Botox, then why shouldn't we?"

"Botox?" She leaned forward and examined the corners of my eyes. "Summer, have you had Botox treatments?"

"No!" I laughed. "I did buy a good eye cream last year that I've been using. Does that count? Although I bought it at the grocery store, so I'm not sure that puts me in a league with those who really attempt to fight the forces of gravity."

"I don't even use an eye cream, and I should. I know I don't pamper myself enough. It's not part of my thinking. Time to make a change, though, don't you think?"

I nodded and dipped my spoon into the rich pudding. Before I had swallowed the decadently delicious dessert, I grinned.

"What is it? What are you thinking?"

The pudding slid down my throat in the most soothing sort of way. "I was thinking of a joke I heard about a woman who is eating her way through a box of chocolates. She says, 'I don't dare try to lose weight at my age. Can you imagine how many wrinkles I'd suddenly have if all my cellulite went away? Besides, bonbons are better than Botox. They fill in the wrinkles and taste good too.'"

"Clever! And don't forget that bonbons don't require a needle for application."

I laughed, and we continued to enjoy our dessert with no regrets.

"You know," Noelle said, "since we're on the topic of self-improvement, I was reading an article a few weeks ago that made it sound as if every third woman in America was having some sort of cosmetic work done to her face or body."

"That might be. I don't know. I'm not the one in three."

"The article also said that one in four women have breast cancer. Can you believe that? One in four. I had no idea the numbers were that high. What do you think the reason is? Did you do a lot of research on it when your mom was going through all that?"

My spirit quieted itself and drew inward. "No, not a lot."

Noelle must have sensed my immediate climate change. She reached across the table and squeezed my hand. "I'm sorry. That was insensitive of me to toss out the comment about your mom. I didn't mean to bring you down."

"You didn't. It's just that…" I stopped myself before confiding to her any details of the pending biopsy. I was determined to stay in denial.

Just then her cell phone rang. Noelle took the call with a quick apology, stepping away from the table. Not that it would have mattered since she was speaking in Dutch. The break in our conversation couldn't have come at a better time.

Would I have enjoyed the extraordinary field of tulips as much as I had that morning if thoughts of my health had been at the forefront of my mind?

No.

Pressing health issues would still be pressing health issues one week from now when I returned home. For now, all I wanted was to live in the moment. I wanted to soak up the beauty of this place and the new experiences and just be happy.

The waiter brought the check to the table, and I pulled out my credit card before Noelle returned. I hoped it worked the same way as at home. Noelle had been paying for everything so far; I wanted to pitch in.

She returned to the table as I was signing the credit card receipt.

"What do you think you're doing, young lady?"

"Trying to figure out where to write in the tip. And don't you dare try to stop me."

"Oenie."

"Oenie moonie looney tooney," I retorted.

She laughed. "I only make up new words. You make up entire rhymes. Impressive!" Noelle reached into her purse and pulled out a few coins. "I'll let you pay this time but only because you're being such a poet about it. I'll cover the tip. We're not big tippers here."

A half grin pulled up the side of my mouth. "If you're paying some and I'm paying some, does that make our lunch a Dutch treat?"

For a moment Noelle appeared as if she didn't understand my little joke. "You can stop trying to find all the possible connections to things Dutch, if you want. I think we might have exhausted enough stereotypes for one day."

"Got it."

On the way home we stopped at a grocery store that seemed similar to any grocery store at home except this one was smaller, and of course all the prices were in euros and the labels in Dutch. Noelle selected a variety of fresh vegetables and the usual basics, such as eggs, bread, and milk. She added some interesting bottles to the cart, explaining that it was drinkable yogurt.

"This is what Jelle usually has for breakfast. It's okay, but I would rather eat yogurt with a spoon or, better yet, frozen. Do you want to try one?"

I selected chocolate and said I would give it a whirl at breakfast the next morning.

"Actually, we're not going to have breakfast at home tomorrow."

"Is that your surprise for me?"

"It's part of the surprise. We're going to start early in the morning. Very early."

"How early?"

Noelle squinted her eyes. "Four o'clock."

I couldn't imagine what sort of surprise required rising at four a.m. "Do we have to drive far?"

"Not too far. I think you'll like it. I hope you'll like it. It's a very special place, and that's all I'm going to say. You're not going to get any more clues from me." She pantomimed zipping her lips shut.

"How about if I take the bottle of yogurt with me just in case I'm not crazy about the surprise? Then at least I can have something else to look forward to."

Noelle shook her head at my comment but didn't respond. She led the way to the checkout, where she chatted with the young woman at the register. It amazed me to watch her converse fluently in Dutch. Her expressions and inflections were the same as when she spoke in English, but she used a bunch of words that seemed to start in a different place in her throat. Certain back-of-the-throat sounds and tongue-flicking-off-the-roof-of-the-mouth sounds weren't used with English words. Her ease as a bilingual person baffled me. I had taken three years of German in high school, but if my life depended on it, I bet I could come up with only five or six words now.

Watching Noelle, I was sure there had to be something to the necessity of using a second language regularly or the words would just slip out of your memory. At least that was the case for me.

Once we were back at Noelle's, she and I worked together in her kitchen, washing vegetables and cutting them up for steaming later. She put some rice in an electric rice cooker and let it do its thing for the next hour.

With a comfortable stretch of time available to us before Jelle returned home for dinner, Noelle pulled out the shortbread cookie tin where she had stored my letters for several decades. We made a pot of tea and sat on the living room couch, reading all the letters together.

"Look at this one with the sad face," Noelle said. "This was your dentist-day letter."

"Let me see." I looked at the unfolded piece of stationery with the printed pony in the corner. I remembered that stationery. My grandmother had given it to me in seventh grade. At the top I had entitled the letter "Dentist Day."

"I'll read it to you." Noelle put on a pair of reading glasses and began, "Dear Pen Pal." Looking at me over the rim of the glasses, she said, "That's me."

"Yes," I agreed, playing along with the dramatization and sipping my mint tea.

"This may be the last letter you ever receive from me. That is, the last letter you receive from the me who has crooked teeth. My father took me to the dentist after school today, and I might be getting braces. Yes, braces! My life is about to end!"

"Did I really write that?"

Noelle held up the evidence and pointed to the margin. "Yes, you did. And see the frowny face you drew? So cute."

I groaned. "And to think that I accused our three girls of being drama queens! Now I know where they got it. Please don't ever show that to my girls. They would never let me live it down."

"Wait," Noelle said playfully. "There's more."

"I'm sure there is."

Noelle focused back on the letter. "I can already guess that *he* is going to call me 'Brace Face' or 'Metal Mouth.' *He* called Missy Heinrich 'Tin Grin' when she got her braces. You do know who I'm talking about, don't you? Tommy Driscoll."

"Oh, Tommy." I swooned. "I forgot all about Tommy Driscoll. Now he owns a Toyota dealership in Akron. At least that's what I heard. I haven't seen him since our ten-year high school reunion. Oh boy, did I ever have a crush on Tommy. A big crush. But he never noticed me. Not even when I got my braces. I only hoped he would call me one of those names. At least he called Missy names. He just ignored me."

"I always wanted braces," Noelle said. "I thought they looked cool. I remember taking a paper clip once and bending it to fit around my front teeth so it would look as if I had braces. I wore it to the grocery store with my mom and kept my lips closed the whole time so she wouldn't see it. There was only one problem."

"What?"

"The sharp end of the paper clip jammed into my gums, and as soon as I tasted the blood, I wanted to spit it out. So I did, right there on the floor in the frozen-food aisle. My mother was livid.

She made me go report to the grocery clerk that I had made a mess. They sent a guy over with a bucket of water and a mop. Complete overkill for a little puddle of spit. 'Cleanup on aisle four' and all that."

I gave her a sympathetic look.

"Would you like more tea? I'm going to make some more. This has gone cold. I probably should have made coffee. That would have been more typical, but tea sounded good."

She was in the kitchen, filling the electric kettle with more water, so I turned my attention back to the Dentist Day letter and read the rest of what I had written to her.

"This is the cutest part," I called into the kitchen.

"Is there another little drawing?"

"No. What's cute is the way I signed it. I wrote, 'Your friend until the end of time or until I die of braces-humiliation.' Of course I spelled 'humiliation' wrong. Then I wrote my whole name, as if you might possibly mix me up with some other girl named Summer who was writing pen pal letters to you."

"We both did that for a long time, didn't we? We signed our whole names." Noelle returned with fresh tea bags on a small serving plate.

"Oh, look at this one." I pulled from the tin a letter written on lined notebook paper with a hand-drawn picture of a Christmas tree in the corner and a string of snowflakes trailing down the side margins. "I don't remember this one."

"Read it," Noelle said.

I skimmed through the particulars of the letter I had written over Christmas vacation during my freshman year in high school: a visit from my grandparents from Minnesota, a sled run the neighborhood boys built, and how my little brother had his tonsils out and begged me to play Monopoly with him once he was feeling better.

I felt both strange and comforted, reading through a trail of my life history while we sipped mint tea. In my waffling back and forth between denial and mental preparation for my days soon to be altered and possibly cut short, I thought of how going through these captured images of my past was similar to "my life flashed before my eyes," as the saying goes. Only this wasn't a flash. It was a stroll in the company of a close friend while holding a cup of tea. Was this part of God's tender care for me?

My conclusion at the end of the day was that I had lived a blessed life. I went to bed with that thought pressed to the forefront of my mind. I had lived a fairly typical life, with its share of ups and downs, but I couldn't deny that God had been good to me.

Once the light was turned off and I was under the comforter, my thoughts weren't on the fear of the unknown future but on the unfolded past. I felt grateful.

Closing my eyes, I tried to pull up a mental image of the endless field of tulips. I don't usually dream in color, but that night I'm pretty sure I did.

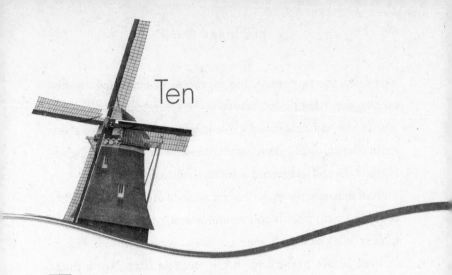

Ten

The next morning Noelle tapped on my guest room door at four o'clock. I already was awake and sitting up in bed, propped against the pillows, reading from the devotion book.

"Can you be ready in half an hour or less?"

"No problem."

The night before, she had prepared me for the surprise trip by saying I should wear layers and not the nicest clothing I had brought but to lean toward comfort over fashion. Those hints didn't help me a bit in trying to decode what adventure lay ahead. Nor did the wardrobe suggestions help much in deciding what to wear. I had packed a few pairs of pants, one skirt, several shirts, and two sweaters. I went for the dark brown pants, white button-up blouse, and brown pullover sweater.

At the dinner table the night before, while Noelle spoke to Jelle in code, I figured out a few clues. He knew where we were going and what we were doing, but Noelle wanted to make sure she didn't give away any hints to me.

She could have conversed with Jelle in Dutch; that would

have been the easy route. But Noelle had mentioned my first evening there that since everyone in the family spoke English and Dutch, she had established a rule long ago that whenever guests in their home didn't speak Dutch, everyone would speak English. She said she still had memories of how isolated she felt in her early years of marriage when she was trying so hard to learn Dutch but couldn't keep up with conversations around the family dinner table at Jelle's parents' home.

Just before four-thirty, in the predawn chill, Noelle and I climbed into Bluebell as quietly as we could, since the neighborhood still was sleeping. She handed me the bottle of drinkable yogurt and smiled. "You wanted this for backup, right?"

"That depends. Will I need it as a backup, or are we going to eat breakfast?"

"We'll get some breakfast. Don't worry. I haven't allowed a single houseguest to starve yet." She started the engine and bit her lower lip as if the sudden noise of the car could have somehow been muffled.

"I think I know where we're going." I buckled my seat belt. "I figured it out."

"Oh, you did, did you? Where do you think we're going?"

"To the harbor to see where Jelle works." I thought my conclusion was quite clever.

Noelle scrunched up her nose. "That would not be my idea of a surprise. Don't get me wrong. I admire my husband greatly for what he does, but I could never do it."

At our dinner the previous night, over plates of steamed carrots and broccoli, I had found out more about Jelle's job. He worked for a large company that outfitted huge ships that came into Rotterdam Harbor. Some of the fishing vessels were the size of small villages and came from around the world, each arriving in need of provisions.

Jelle and his division of the company supplied the ships. He had told stories at dinner of how some captains would hand Jelle's employees a list in Japanese or Sudanese, and they would have to translate the list and hunt down the supplies. Needs on board could be as simple as one hundred kilos of ground coffee or as complex as a random part for a broken computer that was discontinued in 1993 or a chain saw with a certain type of blade.

Jelle and his staff managed to fulfill the requests, sometimes at the last minute, and off the ship would sail. He made his job sound so interesting that I said something along the lines of how fascinating it would be to visit one of the ships.

Noelle had cast a wary glance at me across the table. "It's a lot rougher than he is making it sound. Jelle spends most of his time in the office on the phone or on the computer. He doesn't go on board that often. But I can tell you, salty crews man the ships that come into harbor. I've only gone on board with him once. I never let the girls go with him."

"You make it sound like Tortuga from *The Pirates of the Caribbean*."

Jelle laughed at my comparison. Noelle didn't laugh. She had pressed forward in the conversation, saying we only had a few days to spend together. She listed our schedule as a day in Amsterdam, a visit to Haarlem, and a possible jaunt to Delft.

"Delft is not far from here. We could go for half a day, if you like. But if we do all that, it doesn't leave a day for going to the harbor."

With her adamant disdain at going to the harbor still lingering from last night's conversation, I leaned back in the passenger seat of little Bluebell as she hummed along the nearly vacant road. "So you're not driving to the harbor, I take it."

"No."

"I thought maybe all your disagreeable comments about the harbor last night were made to throw me off track."

She shook her head. "What we're doing today is exactly what we need to do today, and that's all I'm going to tell you. Relax. This is going to be a good day. You'll like my surprise. I just know it."

I had to tease her. "Will I love it as much as I loved your surprise CD yesterday?"

"More." She didn't say much else until we arrived at what looked like a car repair shop. After pulling up in front of the closed garage, she turned off the engine. "Here we are."

"A garage? We're spending the day at a garage?"

"You oenie, come on."

Dramatically I gripped the door handle. "I refuse to go until you assure me that this surprise of yours has nothing to do with car parts, brake fluid, or anything else auto related."

Noelle laughed. "You really are more paranoid than I realized."

"You think I'm joking? Going to a car parts store is my husband's idea of an afternoon out together. Oh, and he usually throws in a stop at the giant hardware store so we can look at drill bits and PVC pipe."

"Fear not, Summer. No motor oil or drill bits will be used in our upcoming adventure. And since I have no idea what a PVC pipe is, I'm pretty sure that can be taken off the list as well."

"So, exactly what are we doing?"

"You don't like surprises much, do you?" Noelle looked astonished to discover this truth about me.

"What was your first clue?"

"You are so afraid. Don't be frightened." She studied my expression as if she still couldn't understand where my strong hesitancy was coming from. "If it will give you peace, I will tell you that we are leaving Bluebell here in capable hands, and you and I are walking a little ways to a..." She hesitated.

I reached over and gripped the door handle again, indicating she would have a hard time making me budge unless she provided full disclosure.

"We're walking to a train station. All right? Is that helpful enough for you? The station is not far. Wait here a minute. I have to fill out a paper and put the key in the overnight box."

Soon Noelle returned and opened my door, letting all the cold morning air into the car. "Are you ready, Summer Breeze?"

"We could use a summer breeze right now. A warm summer breeze!" I eased out of the car and buttoned up my coat. "It's so cold!"

"Yes, but it's not snowing. Or raining. Our short walk will warm us up."

I suspected her idea of short was going to be different from my idea of short.

I followed her down a narrow alleyway with the buildings on either side shadowing our path and making it feel as if we were sneaking about in the middle of the night rather than being extremely early birds. We turned left and trekked passed a number of shops on a street that had fourteen letters in its name.

As I kept up with Noelle, I realized her quick stride seemed to come from more than the slightly longer length of her legs. I suspected she walked a lot. The street we were traversing had narrow concrete walkways in front of the shops, but the street itself was cobblestone. We crossed to the other side on the uneven cobblestones, and Noelle seemed an equally brisk walker, no matter what the terrain.

We entered a small shop that was the only one on the block with lights on inside. As soon as Noelle opened the door, I knew where we were. We were in a bakery. Oh, the fragrance of fresh-baked bread on a crisp morning! What a universally welcoming scent.

Noelle ordered a lot. She bought four round loaves of bread, a variety of pastries, and two dozen small, round butter cookies.

She turned to me and asked something, but she still was speaking in Dutch, so I had no idea what she said.

After realizing the language blip, she shook her head. "Would you like anything to eat now?"

"One of those." I pointed at a flaky-looking round pastry that had half of an apricot baked into it.

Noelle ordered two of them along with two koffies. I figured out she was ordering mine with lots of hot milk. We took our early-morning bounty with us and ventured back into the new day's chill.

"Are we going to eat these on the train?" I caught a whiff of the dark coffee I held in a takeout cup.

"Yes. We need to walk fast enough to get on this next train. Otherwise we'll have to wait forty minutes for the next one. The train stop is just down that way. We should be able to make it."

We did. Noelle and I stood on the platform with armfuls of white paper parcels that wrapped up her generous bread purchases. Obviously she had bought more than she and I could eat, but I still didn't know to whom she would deliver this daily bread.

The train station was more of a stop than a station because all it consisted of was a platform and a machine where Noelle purchased tickets for us. I'd never been on a real train, and I told her so.

"Trains are a lifesaver here. I prefer taking the train most of the time, if I can avoid driving in traffic. Or paying for parking. And don't get me started on the skyrocketing price of petrol. We pay twice what you pay in the U.S. Sometimes more. So the next time you want to complain about your gas prices, just remember what I'm paying."

The train rolled in on time. It felt good to enter the warm train car. I was surprised at how many early-morning passengers were already on board. We sat in fabric-covered seats facing each other and pulled out a small folding shelf to hold our coffee.

I swallowed my first bite of the apricot pastry. "Delicious. The coffee is good too."

"This was a good choice." Noelle held up her matching pastry.

"So how far are we going?"

"Not far." Her smile was soon leveled when she took another bite of the pastry.

"You're enjoying this way too much."

"Yes, I am. My girls say it's a sickness. I call it my hobby. I love planning surprises. I managed to pull off several quite-memorable birthday parties for the two of them, thank you very much. Tara's sixteenth was the best." She grinned as if savoring the memory's sweetness as much as I was savoring the pastry's sweetness.

That small confession helped me to understand why this surprise was so important to Noelle. It also made me realize that if I wasn't particularly crazy about the surprise, whatever it was, I should still act appreciative since this was such a joyful hobby for her. Or a sickness, depending on whose side I ended up agreeing with once the day was over.

The train rolled past a lineup of brick homes, and then we came to the end of the uniform neighborhood houses. A marshy stretch beside a canal ran parallel with the train track. Light had tiptoed in while I was sipping the coffee and looking out the window. It was morning. A few people on bikes pedaled by on the smooth trail that ran like a plumb line along the narrow canal. They seemed to be heading into town, and we were heading out into the country.

I nodded off a little, lulled by the train's movement and the satisfying sensation of a warmed and sugared-up belly.

The station where we disembarked had a sign with a name I

didn't even try to pronounce. We were definitely in the country. I felt as if I had awakened in a fairy tale. The houses near the train platform looked as if they had been there for two hundred years. Hansel and Gretel could have strolled out of any of the charming cottages, and I wouldn't have been surprised. Or perhaps here it would be Hans and Greta.

The first cottage we walked past had an honest-to-goodness Dutch door. Both the top and bottom sections were closed that morning. I could imagine the maid of the house opening the top portion on a summer day and leaning halfway out in her apron-covered dress, conversing with passersby.

"This is like an illustration in a book of fables," I said.

"You like it?"

"Yes."

Noelle's eyes twinkled. "Good. I knew you would. We don't have far to walk. How are you doing?"

"I'm fine." The air felt clean and crisp but didn't give my lungs a shiver as the earlier chill in the air had.

Noelle picked up the pace, and I offered to carry some of her bread loaves. We split the bounty and continued our journey away from the town and toward a gathering of trees. A young woman in jeans and a long sweatshirt stood by the side of the road, softly singing a popular song in English. She held a rope tethered to a calf. Evidence of where the piped-in music came from rose from her sweatshirt pocket and connected in each of her ears.

Noelle gave her half a nod. I did the same. The young woman didn't change her expression. She seemed to be going about what she did every day of her life in the country. I had heard my kids playing the same pop tune before, but I could never imagine any of my children singing it while standing by the side of the road with a calf on a rope.

"What sort of parallel universe have you taken me to?"

"You really are allergic to suspense, aren't you?" Her tone was partially compassionate and partially ribbing.

"Yes, I am allergic to suspense. And if you don't clue me in pretty quickly, I might have an allergic reaction right here. And I can't guarantee that it will be attractive."

"You're so funny, Summer. Be patient. We're almost there. Honest. I don't want to spoil it for you. Just a bit farther."

Eleven

Noelle led the way down a tree-lined road and across a retractable sort of bridge. The bridge arched over the canal but appeared as if it could be pulled back to either side if a small boat needed the extra headroom to motor past it.

"My father-in-law once told me that he could take me anywhere I wanted to go in Holland by boat. I never took him up on the offer, but I wish I had. Water runs through this country like lifeblood through veins."

At that moment my veins were feeling the pulse of Noelle's brisk pace. We probably had walked only a mile, but she had made it a fast mile.

"Are we going to your father-in-law's farm? Is that what's at the end of this lane?"

Noelle stopped walking. She turned and looked at me with an expression of disappointment. "You guessed."

As soon as I saw her shoulders slump, I wished I hadn't figured it out. She was having so much fun keeping me going. I realized something important about myself in that moment. I like to be in control. Trying to manage a large family can have that effect on a person.

But that was more of a convenient excuse for my anxious need to have all the details up-front. At the foundation of my need for control was the thought that it was up to me to make things run smoothly or at least to make them go the way I wanted them to go. I'm sure that's why I was so quick to put aside scheduling the biopsy. I wanted to be in control, even if the only control I had was when the results would be presented to me.

As is often the case when I'm suddenly confronted with an undeniable truth, I felt embarrassed. Not embarrassed so much for popping out the rather obvious summation that we were going to a farmhouse and therefore it must be her father-in-law's. I was embarrassed by my need to be in control. If Noelle's hobby was surprising people, my hobby was having everything organized and neatly controlled.

That embarrassed me because I knew that in many cases controlling could be the opposite of trusting. Why wasn't I able to just go along with Noelle on this surprise? Did I have any reason not to trust her?

The same line of logic applied to why I had dodged the biopsy and delayed the testing. Did I have any reason not to trust God?

"Are you okay, Summer?"

I nodded. "I'm sorry."

"For what?"

"For spoiling your surprise."

She brushed away my apology. "Actually, this farm used to belong to my father-in-law, but it's been transformed quite a bit since he lived here. Come, you'll see."

I fell into step with Noelle but found it difficult to be as carefree about the path of denial that had brought me on a lark to the Netherlands. Now that I had figured out this small piece about my hobby of controlling, I felt bad.

Where was God in all this? What was He doing in my life? I really had no idea. I was pretty sure I didn't trust Him as much as I had a short week ago when long life and comfort seemed to be the path stretched out before me.

We exited the tree-lined lane, and ahead of us sat a farmhouse built of brick with white-framed windows. The roof appeared to be equal in space and size to the house it topped. A single brick chimney rose at the back of the roof, and a large white bird perched on the roof near the chimney.

The bird took flight as we approached. Noelle stopped walking. "Isn't it quaint? Here's the whole story. This is my in-laws' old farmhouse, as you guessed. But my sister-in-law lives here now, and she has turned this into a… Oh dear, I don't remember the word. A community?"

I waited for her to elaborate. It would be nice to know if I was about to walk into a club or a cult. "What sort of community?"

"Women come and live here, and they work the farm together."

"So it's a female-only commune?"

"No, not like a hippie commune. It's a spiritual community."

"Is it a cult?"

"No, no. I'm not explaining it the right way. The women have regular prayer and worship times. It's not a nunnery, though, if that's what you're thinking. It's beautiful. You'll see. I don't know how to explain it, but I want you to experience this. Fresh. Without any preconceived concepts."

"Okay."

Having just confronted myself on my apparent need to control, I was trying to let go and be more trusting. It almost seemed as if God had set me up by letting me catch a glimpse of my fear and desire to control before presenting me with this out-of-the-ordinary opportunity to step into a new situation where I had no control. I was at the mercy of Noelle for translation as well as direction.

We approached the front door, a Dutch door painted green. Noelle pressed on the latch and opened it without knocking. To my surprise we entered the kitchen and not the living room. Everything around us looked clean and tidy as well as quite old-fashioned and out-of-date.

The first thing we heard was singing. It was wonderful. The harmonies were beautiful.

Noelle put her finger to her lips, and we stayed tucked in the kitchen's corner. In a whisper to me she said, "It's the Doxology. They are finishing morning devotions. I had hoped we would be here in time to eat with them. We'll have lunch here. That's when they have the main meal of the day."

The singing ended while Noelle was whispering to me. We could hear the women in the adjoining room rustling and rising from the table. Noelle stepped closer to the opening between the kitchen and the dining area and leaned her head in.

An enthusiastic woman who appeared to be well past her sixties greeted Noelle. The woman's blond hair was pulled back in a short ponytail at the nape of her neck. She was wearing a knotted floral scarf. Her complexion was a picture of health and energy. I thought she was stunning.

"Hannah, this is Summer. Summer, I would like you to meet my sister-in-law."

We exchanged smiles and nods. Hannah welcomed me with a deep voice, which surprised me. I would have imagined an airy voice from a woman who looked to be such a picture of health. Her gaze had a penetrating and calming effect.

"You are welcome here." Her accent was heavy. I got the impression she wasn't fluent in English, and that only made me wish all the more that I could speak Dutch. Even if all I said was "Thank you." I couldn't remember how to say it, although I had heard it many times.

Maybe I was willing to reenroll in Dutch language school.

Noelle and Hannah conversed in Dutch as some of the other women entered the kitchen, carrying the breakfast dishes. Several of them were happy to see Noelle, which was obvious by their greetings. They kissed on the cheek three times. First on the right side, then the left, then the right side again. It was the warmest greeting I'd seen yet and gave me a bit of understanding into something Noelle had told me about—how a close friend receives more honor and warmer treatment than an acquaintance or a neighbor.

Noelle was definitely an honored friend among these women.

For the next hour or so I just stood back and contentedly fit in wherever it seemed natural. I counted a total of eleven women, and they all knew their assignments and went about the morning chores with a light spirit.

One of the women tried to converse with me in English. She told me she was from Poland and had only been here a few weeks. Her questions were understandable to me, but I could tell she couldn't understand my responses. It didn't matter. We used hand gestures, pointed, and nodded. Communication, it seems, is the sum of all its parts and not limited to only the expression of familiar words.

I felt included in the tightly knit circle and had no problem picking up a dishtowel and drying the breakfast dishes alongside one of the other women.

Noelle came over and linked her arm in mine. "You and I have a chore to do. We're going out to the barn."

"I hope it doesn't involve beasts of burden."

"It involves one chicken."

"I did tell you that I'm a city girl, didn't I?" I walked with Noelle out the Dutch door and around the side of the house. Across a flat stretch of freshly turned soil stood a slightly dilapidated-looking barn.

"This is just the place for city girls."

"And why is that?"

"You are afraid of too many things, Summer. You are afraid of what you don't know and what you can't see. This doesn't make sense to me because you are so brave in many other ways."

Feeling as if she had just revealed one of my weak spots when I wasn't ready to talk about it, I grabbed on to her positive comment and said, "In what ways do you think I'm brave?"

Noelle pulled back slightly, as if the answer to my question should be obvious. "You adopted two daughters from Korea and then took in two foster boys who have caused you significant challenges. I never could have done that."

The way our family came together never had seemed like a courageous thing to me. It seemed normal. Wayne and I did it together.

"You were also brave to book this trip and come on the spur of the moment."

I didn't want to tell her that my decision was born of anxiety and denial rather than courage.

"I promise you'll only have to be a little brave when you come into the barn with me. I also promise it will be good for you. You'll see."

As we approached, I knew by the stench coming from the barn that more than one chicken inhabited this domain. My eyes adjusted to the darkness inside, and I soon saw that we were in the presence of a variety of beasts.

"I thought you said this chore involved only one chicken?"

"It does. You!"

I gave Noelle's arm a playful pinch. She was enjoying this far too much. I had never picked up from her letters what a mischievous person she was. At least I preferred to think of all this as playful and not menacing.

"Since when did I ask you to be my life coach?"

Noelle lowered her chin and said in a solemn voice, "Ever since we were in the third grade. You motivate me, and I motivate you. That's how it works. That's how it's always worked."

I noticed one of the women seated on a small three-legged stool next to the only cow in the barn. She said something to Noelle, and Noelle countered in English, "Yes, that's why we came out here. Summer would like to help you milk the cow."

"No I wouldn't."

"Yes you would."

I gave her a scowl.

Noelle's strength wasn't to be underestimated. The strength in her arms and legs was nothing compared to the strength in her will and especially in the expressive scowl her face had taken on in response to mine.

"Summer, you need to try to milk the cow. This is the opportunity offered you today. Take it. Don't be afraid."

I can't explain what happened inside me when I heard Noelle's admonition. That's what it was. Not a scold or a challenge. It was an admonition. An invitation to step out of my controlled biosphere and live a little. She was more right than she knew.

"Okay." I said the word slowly, but I said it. When I did, I felt as if I opened a gate inside my spirit. As long as that gate had been closed, I was the one who had control of who or what went in and out. When I opened the invisible gate, I was saying to God, *I'm open. Open to whatever You bring in or out. I'm open to all of life.*

The other woman rose slowly from the stool. Speaking to the cow in a low voice, she ran her hand across its side. Apparently the cow spoke Dutch, because she remained content and merely flicked her tail back and forth at the gathering of flies.

Once I was seated, I looked up at Noelle. "This cow is huge."

She broke into a wide grin.

Not only did the cow appear huge from my vantage point, but it also smelled. I held my breath, thinking how livestock scent is something that must take a long time to become acclimated to.

The other woman leaned over and motioned for me to place my hands in the obvious locale to coax the milk into the bucket. I wasn't prepared for how warm it felt. "This is way out of my comfort zone, just so you know."

"I know," Noelle said flippantly. "Go ahead. Milk the cow."

I tried squeezing, but nothing happened. My hands-on instructor put her hands on top of mine. She had the largest, strongest, roughest female hands I had ever felt. She started both my hands in the correct position, and together we squeezed and pulled, and the metal bucket began to fill once again with milk. Warm milk. The fragrance of the milk was slightly sweet. That surprised me too.

I laughed aloud. Too loud. The cow flinched, and I thought she was going to kick me.

My barnyard instructor quickly calmed the cow and me with her soothing voice and put me back on task. She then took her able hands and positioned my shoulder and my head so I was pressed right against the cow. The proximity seemed to have a relaxing effect on the cow but not on me.

All I could think was, *I am hugging a cow. Why am I hugging a cow?* I'd need to wash my hair and my clothes the first opportunity I had.

A few more minutes into the process, I began to relax. I could feel the rhythm. There was a steadiness to this simple task that was similar to the ongoing beat in a song. I say "simple" task, but I knew that if I hadn't had such aggressive direction, I still would be skittish, and the cow would probably be the same.

"This is pretty amazing," I said a few moments later. My voice was more soothing than it had been earlier. "I feel very organic. I need to have a piece of straw hanging out the side of my mouth."

Noelle smiled. "I wish I had my camera. You're a little Dutch barn maid."

"I don't think I'll need a picture to remember that I did this."

"It's pretty cool doing things you wouldn't normally do, isn't it?"

My smile was the answer Noelle seemed to have hoped for from the time she had set up this surprise excursion.

"The next time you face something new that you think you don't want to do, remember this moment, Summer. Remember this feeling. You can do all things through Christ, who strengthens you."

I didn't look over at Noelle. I kept my bleary eyes fixed on the milk bucket and my shoulder pressed against the agreeable cow. The cow that I was hugging. The cow that seemed to be hugging me back.

I can do all things through Christ, who strengthens me. Even chemotherapy.

I cleared my throat quietly and asked Noelle, "Where is that verse?"

"Philippians. The fourth chapter, I think. You've heard it before, right?"

"Yes, many times before, I'm sure. I've probably even memorized it at some point. But I want to hold on to it."

"Hold on to it?"

"You know what I mean. I want to remember it. There's a difference for me between memorizing something and really holding on to it in my heart."

"Ah." Noelle's voice softened. "You want to own the truth and not just rent the words."

"Yes. Yes, that's it exactly. I want to own the truth of that verse. I have merely rented some of God's words for far too long. The time has come for me to own them."

I pressed my cheek against the tolerant cow and wondered how much it would cost me to own words that God wrote in His own blood.

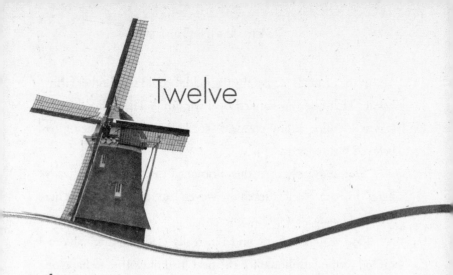

Twelve

Lunch with all the women was my favorite part of our time at the farm community. I called the women "sisters" when Noelle and I were working side by side, hanging freshly washed sheets on the clothesline.

"They're not exactly sisters, as in the usual perception of women who wear habits and make vows," Noelle said. "Some of them are more on the free-spirited side than you might imagine. They're actually more like Sisterchicks."

"That works."

"It does, doesn't it? I've always thought of you and me as more than friends or pen pals. We're Sisterchicks too, aren't we?"

"Definitely. Sisterchicks forever!" I liked that term for our unique friendship. We were sisters at heart, but in moments like this we clearly had a bit of a "chick" side to us that hadn't diminished even though we were strolling down the corridors of midlife.

I stood back and looked at the sheets hanging on the line, the farmhouse with its unusual, wide roof, and the large tree that stood between the two of them and was all afluff in pink blossoms.

In the distance, across the flat field, I could see another farm-house. That one was flanked by a windmill. The pastoral scene was as soothing as any postcard Noelle had ever sent me of her beloved Netherlands.

"You know what? At this moment I can't believe I'm really here," I said as Noelle tucked the woven laundry basket under her arm and balanced it on her hip.

"You really are here, and I'm really glad you are." She returned to the farmhouse for the next load of clothes to hang on the line.

I stayed in the yard, crossed my arms in front of me for warmth, and composed a little thank-you note to God. I told Him how grateful I was for Noelle, my one-of-a-kind friend.

Then I told Him I thought the world He made was beauti-ful. Not only the tulips but also the sky; the pink, blossoming tree; the spring green grass. Even the big, smelly, dear cow. How amaz-ing was it that God could take green grass, put it through a brown cow, and give us white milk?

At home I rarely felt caught up in the wonder of such simple elements of life. Getting away had not only expanded my view of God and His world but also, thanks to the admonitions of my Sisterchick, my view of myself.

A few hours later, when we gathered at the long wooden table in the dining room for the main meal of the day, I still was feel-ing the same closeness to the Lord as when I was outside standing by the clothesline.

We bowed our heads to give thanks before the meal. Several

of the women prayed. I couldn't understand their words, but I did understand the gratefulness in their hearts. In an uncharacteristic expression of spontaneity, I prayed aloud as well.

As we passed the large bowls of chicken soup with boiled potatoes, carrots, and celery, a lovely closeness encircled us around the table. The bread Noelle had purchased at the bakery that morning was a big hit, as were the cookies, which were set aside to make their afternoon koffie time more special.

The food was delicious. Everything tasted fresh and whole-some, with most of the ingredients grown on the farm and then canned or frozen.

One of the women, a timid brunette who sat directly across from me, had bruises on her face and cuts on her forearms. I tried not to make it obvious that I was watching her, but I'm not sure how well I did. She ate her meal like no one I had ever seen. She took each sip of soup with an expression of expectation. Each swallow was savored, as if she had never tasted chicken soup before. When the first bite of the bread went into her mouth, she closed her eyes and seemed to let the morsel melt on her tongue. She kept murmuring words that sounded like adulations of praise. I realized that she appreciated the meal more than I have appreci-ated most things in my life—large or small.

Watching her was a distinct pleasure because the meal was an act of worship for her. Even though I'm sure I've appreciated a number of meals over the years, I couldn't recall ever entering into the experience with the same sort of eagerness to receive each ounce of the sensations, tastes, and textures.

I'll never forget that woman and the way she embraced the meal with such gratitude.

The other intensely memorable part of our visit, aside from the cow and the view from the clothesline, was what happened with Hannah when we were getting ready to leave. The farmhouse had a small side room off the dining room. A narrow window over a small desk looked out at the neighboring farm with the windmill and the long stretch of fertile earth.

Hannah motioned for Noelle and me to join her in that tiny office space before we left for our late-afternoon train. She closed the door and looked at me in her disarming way. For a brief moment I felt as if I had been called into the principal's office and was about to be told that our son Derrick was on probation again.

But Hannah's words were good news, not negative. "You are a good friend to Noelle," she said to me in her simple English.

I nodded. "Noelle is a good friend to me too."

"Thank you," Hannah replied.

I nodded again. It would have felt odd saying "You're welcome" to Noelle's sensitive sister-in-law. I smiled and looked at Noelle and then back at Hannah.

Nothing more needed to be said. In Hannah's uncomplicated way, she let me know that my friendship with Noelle all these years had mattered deeply.

We walked back to the train platform at Noelle's usual brisk pace, neither of us saying much. I felt as if I had been transformed in the best way possible. Noelle had known what she was doing when she arranged this surprise, and I had every reason to believe she knew how appreciative I was for the experience.

But I didn't state my gratitude until we were on the train and almost back to the town where we had left Noelle's car. I tried to present my thanks as straightforwardly as Hannah had. Simple, to the point, heartfelt.

As soon as I spoke my thanks, Noelle said, "I knew you would like it."

And that was that. Not a lot of gush—the way similar conversations at home ran their usual course. Now all I had to do was learn how to offer honest criticism, and I would be like Jelle's father, who had been admired for his precise opinions.

I had a feeling our visit to Amsterdam would be a good opportunity for me to try out expressions of a few precise opinions. After all, Amsterdam is known for a few things I felt certain I would have no trouble criticizing.

Our plans for the next day were laid out in an orderly fashion that night. After the previous two amazing days at the tulip field and the farm, I anticipated an equally inspiring day in Amsterdam.

However, the next day it took us longer than expected to leave the house. Once we were in the car, a call came that took us on a grand detour.

Noelle had placed her cell phone in a holder on the dashboard, and we weren't even to the end of her street when the phone vibrated. She pressed a button on her steering wheel and answered in Dutch. This allowed her to answer her phone without taking her hands off the steering wheel. I was impressed.

The woman's voice on the speakerphone was low and sounded frightened or panicked. She spoke a long string of Dutch words, then several short sentences, raising her pitch at the end of each, as if asking a question.

Noelle's expression darkened. She responded with compassionate sounds in between the woman's words. For a moment I wondered if the caller was one of Noelle's daughters, caught up in a dramatic or difficult moment.

The conversation went on for several minutes before Noelle's voice took on a directive sound. She seemed to be giving a list to the woman followed by a firm but tender good-bye.

I waited, glancing at Noelle's face. She still looked concerned. I didn't ask if everything was all right because that part was obvious. Exactly what was wrong, I didn't know.

"Listen, Summer, we need to make an adjustment to our plans. We need to go to The Hague before going to Amsterdam."

"Okay." I wasn't exactly sure what she meant. *She did say, "the hag," didn't she? Why are we going to visit a cranky elderly person?*

To lighten the moment, I spouted my husband's familiar adage: "Sometimes we do what we have to do so we can do what we want to do."

Noelle glanced at me as if what I had said was odd.

It made sense to me.

She put on her car's blinker and changed lanes on the narrow road. We took a turn and headed the opposite direction of the sign that pointed to Amsterdam.

The phone rang again, and Noelle entered into another hands-free conversation as she drove through morning commuter traffic.

Looking out the car window, I watched the skittering clouds gather in small bunches like schoolchildren at recess. The weather looked mild and promising for our tour of Amsterdam. I wondered if this detour would take much time. I hoped I'd be able to go with the flow and not try to force the day in the direction I wanted.

Noelle drove into what looked like a crowded neighborhood where the side-by-side, three-story brick homes were replaced by high-rise apartment buildings. Dull gray concrete sides and uniform, rectangular windows gave the rows of apartments an industrial, depressing appearance.

A young woman stood on the corner with a suitcase in tow. She wore draped, dark clothing. Her hair was completely covered with a white scarf. We waited while a man in a turban got out of a car parked on the street beside us. A woman dressed in a sari with a row of gold bracelets circling both her forearms climbed out of the backseat and took swift, small steps toward the building.

This was obviously an ethnic area, and as much as I hated to admit it, I felt uncomfortable. We have parts of Cincinnati where apartment buildings such as these were built years ago. But I never drive through those areas. Never.

In Ohio I was used to seeing Mennonite and Amish women wear their traditional garb. But those women suggested a cozier, simpler life to me, while a mysterious-looking woman draped in dark fabric and a woman in a sari seemed much more foreign.

Noelle ended what was the third or fourth call she had been on while we were driving. She steered around the parked cars, put

on her blinker, and pulled up at the corner where the woman in
the dark garb stood. The woman leaned over, and I felt as if she
was staring into our car. Now I really was uncomfortable.

Noelle lowered the window on my side of the car with the
control button on her door. She called out something in Dutch,
and the woman approached us, wheeling her suitcase behind her.
To my shock she opened the car's back door, tossed the suitcase
onto the seat, and got in.

Noelle drove off quickly, glancing with a thoughtfully concerned expression at the woman in the rearview mirror. The two
exchanged a few words in Dutch. My heart pounded.

I looked at Noelle and then straight ahead. The woman in
the seat behind me made no further sound. I felt as if I were in the
middle of a spy film. Was Noelle a secret agent of some sort, and
she never had told me?

Noelle said something to the woman, including my name in
the sentence. The next sentence was in English.

"Summer, this is Zahida. She needs a ride to the farm."

I turned around and gave the dark-eyed woman a quick nod.
"Hello."

From the backseat came a softly asked question. Noelle responded. Another few lines were spoken, and then again Noelle's
steady response. Her answer included a word that sounded like
"America" or "American."

The woman then released a tense onslaught of barely whispered words.

What is she saying? Is it about me?

As soon as we came to a stoplight, Noelle finished her many words to the other woman. Then she turned to me. "I'm sorry this is all in Dutch, Summer. I'm sure it's confusing to you. Zahida heard us speaking English, and when I told her you were my friend visiting from America, she became frightened."

"Frightened? Of me?" I cast a wary glance at Noelle but didn't dare look over my shoulder at Zahida.

How can this woman be afraid of me? I am the one who is afraid of her!

"It's because you're an American."

"So are you," I snapped without thinking.

"Yes, but she didn't know that before. We haven't been friends for long. I told her just now that I'm from the U.S. It's okay, Summer. Everything is fine. I'll explain all this later."

We drove a short distance in silence. My heart was still pounding. "Are we driving out to the farm?"

"No."

The light changed, and Noelle turned with both hands on the steering wheel and headed down a short street. "Another friend of mine, Belinda, is going out to the farm this afternoon. Zahida will go with her. We're almost to Belinda's house now."

I tried to find a way of settling into the moment, but I didn't know exactly what I should be doing. I had it in my power to offer Zahida an assuring glance or comforting look, but my heart still was racing at the thought of being so close to someone different from me. Someone who was frightened of me.

I tried to remember what Noelle had said the day before in her admonition to me as we walked to the barn. She said I was afraid of too many things. She was right.

Noelle slowed down in front of a row of small houses. She stopped the car. No place to park was in view, so she left the car double-parked with the keys in the ignition and the engine running.

"I'll be right back," she called to me as she jumped out. "You should be fine here, but if you have to move, just drive around the block."

She reached for the suitcase in the backseat. Zahida got out, and I sat alone in the running car. I looked out the window. Zahida and I shot wary glances at each other before averting our eyes. Noelle whisked her off into the unassuming house.

A moment later Noelle's cell phone rang. I let it ring and kept looking over my shoulder, watching for cars. Several smaller ones scooted around with no problem. Then a van came. A great big van with an impatient driver. His persistent honking didn't draw Noelle out of the house.

Don't be afraid. You can do this.

With my heart racing at near aerobic level, I slipped out the passenger side of the car and hurried around to the driver's side. I avoided eye contact with the van's driver. After sliding into the driver's seat, I studied the stick shift and the control panel. Nothing appeared different from the sort of cars I was used to.

The van driver honked his horn again.

Just then the cell phone rang a second time. I gripped the steering wheel and moved forward nice and slow. My hand must have activated the hidden button that answered the phone because a female voice suddenly filled the car with a greeting in Dutch.

"Ah, hello," I called back to the mystery voice. "Um...Noelle isn't here right now. Do you want to call back?"

"Who is this?" the caller asked.

At that moment I realized I had missed the turn I needed to loop around the block back to where Noelle was. Now I was heading toward the downtown traffic with the impatient van driver bearing down on me.

This was not good. Not good at all.

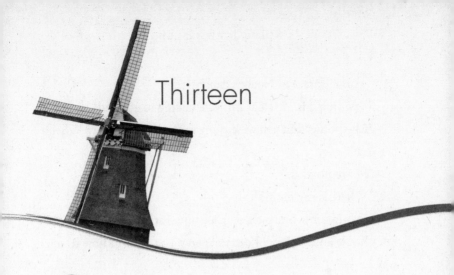

Thirteen

"Get off my tail!" I shouted to the driver of the van that was bearing down on me while I tried to navigate Noelle's car down a narrow street.

"Excuse me? Hello?" the voice on Noelle's cell phone called out.

"Sorry. I, uh…" I couldn't see a place to pull over or to head down another street. I was stuck in the press of the traffic. A bell was consistently chiming, and I realized I hadn't fastened the seat belt. I tried to stabilize the steering wheel with the top of my thigh and slip the seat belt into the slot. I had managed to do a lot of multitasking over the years, but this was a stretch even for me.

"Are you still there?" the female voice asked.

"Yes, I'm still here although I have no idea where *here* is."

"Is this Summer?"

"Yes." Apparently anyone who knew the ins and outs of Noelle's life could come to the speedy conclusion of who the confused American on the other end of the phone call must be.

"This is Tara. I'm Noelle's daughter."

"Yes, Tara! Hi." I felt as if I were talking to a friend.

"My mother said you were going to Amsterdam today. Where are you?"

"I have no idea."

"Where is my mom?"

"I don't know. She picked up a woman and took her to someone's house and…oh no! I can turn now, but I don't know which way to go."

"You're actually driving her car?"

"Yes!"

"Where are you?"

"I'm coming up on a major intersection."

I was out of the neighborhood district and into the thick of traffic. Several options presented themselves to me at once. Before Tara could advise me, I made a split-second decision and turned left, hoping it would allow me to return to the road I was just on.

My theory failed.

The left turn led to another intersection where I had to make another decision, and that left turn led me farther away from where I had started.

"This is very bad. But at least the van is off my tail."

"Can you pull over anywhere?" Tara asked.

"No, I don't see any place to park."

"Then just keep going until you can pull over."

"Okay, but don't hang up, whatever you do."

"Don't worry; I won't."

I followed Tara's instructions and kept driving. For all I knew I was on my way to Belgium!

"Can you describe anything around you?"

I had managed to turn onto a street that didn't have as much traffic. The buildings all looked similar to what I had seen in much of Holland—brick, three stories tall, with rooflines that rose up in a whimsical fashion, as if they had been shaped with a giant cookie cutter. More-modern buildings popped up along the way, but nothing struck me as unique enough to mention as a landmark.

"I think I can turn into a small parking lot here. Yes. I'm turning. It looks like a church. Not an old church, though. It looks new. It has a cross on the top."

I pulled the car into one of the only open spaces.

"Are you safe now?" Tara asked.

"Yes. I'm off the road at least. If I turn off the engine, do you think it will affect the cell phone?"

"No, the phone should stay on. If it doesn't, I'll call back."

I turned off the engine and leaned back, drawing in a deep breath. All I could think at the moment was that Wayne would never believe what I had just done. Whenever we went anywhere, I always let him drive. All the years of being the family taxi driver had sent me into a transporting hiatus. I never tried to navigate new routes at home. This experience was so far out of my comfort zone it was ridiculous.

Tara's voice sounded louder now that the engine was off. "Do you remember anything else my mother said about where you were going?"

"We were planning to go to Amsterdam, but she received a call, and we went the opposite direction. She said we had to stop and see a hag and then—"

"Did she say *'Den Haag'*? That's The Hague. Are you in The Hague now?"

"Oh. Possibly." Obviously, The Hague was a place and not a person. I should have known that.

"If you're in The Hague, the traffic is always difficult. My mother probably took the woman to Belinda's. Did you see a little dog there at the house? A Scottie dog?"

"No, I didn't go inside. I was waiting in the car. We were double-parked, and Noelle said I should drive around the block if I had to move the car. A van came up behind me, and I started driving. That's when you called. But I think I heard the name Belinda earlier in the conversation or when Noelle was on the phone. I don't remember."

"That's okay. This is making more sense. Can you see any street signs or a sign at the church?"

I spelled the words I could see on a sign posted in the parking area. The name of the church was included in what Tara said was a warning that parking was not open to the general public on weekdays. The name of the church was all Tara needed as a clue.

"You are in The Hague, and you are not far from Belinda's. But don't try to drive back to her house. Stay where you are. Even if someone comes and tells you the parking is not for public use, do not leave. I will call Belinda. My mother can come to you more easily than you could drive back to her."

I did as Tara said. I figured out how to hang up the phone, and then I sat alone and waited. I couldn't remember a time when I had felt so out there and isolated, not to mention embarrassed.

How did all that happen? How did I get so far off track so fast? How humiliating! What if Tara hadn't called when she did? I probably would still be driving with that van on my rear bumper. I can't believe I got so lost.

After the first fifteen minutes or so of scolding myself, I leaned back. All I could do was wait. Wait and hope that Noelle found me.

I could hear the steady roar of the city traffic outside the car window. Inside the warm car I was comfortable and calmed. For the first time since I had rushed into the driver's seat, I thought about praying. The first words that came to mind were, *The Lord is my shepherd.*

"And that makes me a little lost sheep," I muttered. I definitely felt like a lost sheep in need of a shepherd. How poetic that the place I had at last found to stop and rest at was a church. The Lord had herded me here. He was protecting me.

I didn't like that image very much. I liked the protection part, of course. I hadn't crashed the car or driven off into the North Sea. But I didn't like feeling lost.

I also didn't feel confident in the driver's seat. It would be easy to draw a lot of life parallels from that thought, but I didn't want to go down that road, so to speak. I was fully aware of my weaknesses and deficiencies. Since I had arrived in the Netherlands, the Lord seemed to find a steady stream of creative ways to make clear to me that He was the One who wanted to be in control of my life.

Am I a slow learner or what?

I rubbed the back of my tensed neck and hoped God wouldn't answer that one. I decided I couldn't do much about the situation. I was here. That's all I knew. Noelle was coming. I would wait. And I would try to think of something other than the humiliation I felt over being stranded.

The tulip fields came to mind. Ah yes. The magnificent, alluring tulips that had unfolded their breathtaking beauty to us in the sunshine. That's what I had hoped this trip to the Netherlands would bring. In moments like the ones we had experienced two days ago, I had found it easy to be at peace and to trust that God had everything under control. I reminded myself that He delighted in creating peace and beauty and in pouring out His love, warmth, and hope on all His creation.

I liked settling into that sort of mind-set with God much more than the scenario in which I was the little lost lamb and He had to carry me around because I was incapable of managing on my own.

For the next twenty minutes I kept watch and waited.

Noelle arrived on foot. She later said she had walked only "a few kilometers." I had seen her walk and knew she could cover a significant stretch of town in a short time.

I gladly turned over the driver's seat to her. She apologized for leaving me in such an awkward situation, and I assured her she didn't need to apologize.

"Did everything turn out okay? With Zahida, I mean?"

"Yes." Noelle nodded. "It's pretty extraordinary. Zahida recently became a Christian."

I hadn't expected Noelle to say that. I turned to face her to make sure I had heard correctly. "She's a Christian? But she was dressed like…"

Noelle waited for me to finish my assumption. I didn't. Obviously I had done just that, made an assumption based on what a woman looked like. Wasn't that a lesson I had sought to teach my children? Why didn't I have that truth rooted in my own heart?

Noelle pulled the car out of the church parking area and skillfully directed us back into the flow of traffic.

Ignoring my unfinished comment, she said, "This morning Zahida told her mother she was a Christian, and she was turned out of their home. I had hoped this wouldn't happen. Do you remember when we went to the tulip fields and I said I had gone last week with a friend, her mother, and her grandmother?"

I nodded.

"That was Zahida. Her mother and grandmother were so enthralled by the tulips. We had a great day together. I had hoped they would be more open-minded when she told them about her decision."

I tried to comprehend what Noelle was saying. This young woman, of whom I was so frightened, was a new Christian. And her family had cut her off. "How terrible for her."

"I know. She's in good hands, though. You saw how Hannah takes in women like Zahida at the farm. It will be a good place for her, and she will be surrounded by other Christians."

I thought of the timid brunette who had sat across from me while we ate lunch and who was so grateful for each bite she took. The women in that home were being taken care of as well as taking care of themselves. Hannah saw to it that they were protected. They were little lost sheep, welcomed into a loving fold.

"What your sister-in-law is doing is amazing."

"I know. That's why I wanted you to experience it. I wanted you to walk into that home without any expectations. That's where Zahida will be by this evening. It will be very good for her. I'm so grateful for Hannah."

I nodded my agreement.

"I have just had an inspiration." Noelle put on her car's blinker. "We'll go to Haarlem instead of Amsterdam. We're close enough, so why not? I have the information on the Ten Boom house. It was a watch shop, correct?"

"Yes."

"Apparently the clock shop is still there, in front of the house. I'm hoping we can take a tour and see where the hiding place was located. I printed out the information, and it is all there in my purse, if you want to pull it out."

I reached to the backseat and removed the folded papers from Noelle's purse.

"You were right about how the Ten Boom family took in Jews as well as those involved in the underground resistance during the occupation years. As a result of their efforts, it's estimated that about eight hundred Jews were spared. That's really something." Noelle shot a glance at me. "Are you okay with doing this instead of going to Amsterdam?"

"Yes, definitely. I much prefer it when you're in the driver's seat."

The traffic let up, and we were in Haarlem sooner than I had expected. I read Noelle the instructions on the papers regarding the parking available in a lot by the train station. The covered parking structure reminded me of the one at the airport.

"Let's hope no out-of-control utility trucks come careening around the corner this time."

"That was a close one, wasn't it?" Noelle said.

She took the papers from me and told me she didn't know exactly where the house was located since she never had been there. At the first street corner, she spotted a sign that said "C. ten Boomhuis," and we were off! Noelle, with her fast-paced stride, and me, puffing to keep up.

We headed for the older part of town, where the buildings became quainter and more photoworthy. I commented on their charm, and Noelle pulled out her camera.

I did the same and enjoyed the approach to the Ten Boom watch shop even more because I was capturing photos of the area and trying to imagine how this corner of Haarlem had looked during the war.

One of the tall, narrow buildings that came into view displayed a sign with a clock on it high above the door. As we walked closer, I saw that the sign read "Ten Boom Museum."

The lower level of the building was a typical, Old-World-style, brick storefront, as I had seen in a number of the towns we had driven through. A long window framed the front of the shop where several people were standing, looking in at the display of watches in the shop.

An alleyway ran down the left side of the building. I paused to gaze at the windows on the second floor that faced the street. They were trimmed in white and stood out against the dull, buttery sandstone brick. Two of the windows were very large and narrow and were topped by a much smaller one directly above them. The housetop slanted inward the way a church spire rises to a point. But instead of a point, this structure rose in the shape of a chimney.

"You okay?" Noelle turned around to come back to where I stood.

"I was trying to imagine what it must have been like, coming here to this place, in search of protection."

Noelle seemed to catch my fervent interest in the Hiding Place for the first time. "Like Zahida going to the farm today."

"Only everything had to be carried out in secret. I can't imagine what it was like during the war."

"I've met many people who lived through it, and you're right. Our generation can't imagine the horror. I hope we can get in on a tour. I didn't make reservations."

I snapped several pictures and caught up with Noelle. Down the alley that ran along the side of the house, we found a green door with the tour times posted.

Noelle checked her watch. "Perfect! The next tour is in five minutes."

Noelle opened the door, and as we entered, my heart swelled with emotion. This was a dream come true. My affection for Corrie ten Boom ran deep. And here I was, entering her home.

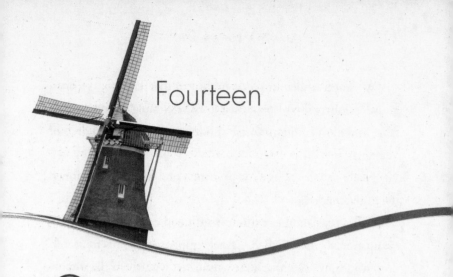

Fourteen

Our tour guide, an older man with laugh lines at the corners of his eyes, led us into the main room above the watch shop. Accompanying Noelle and me were two women from Japan and a couple from South Africa. When all of us said that we spoke English, he seemed pleased to be able to deliver his presentation in only one language.

We formed a small circle and were told how this living room area was the largest place in the house and the spot where the large Ten Boom family would gather. During the occupation this was referred to as the Liberation Room since they were able to assemble here with those they were hiding from the Nazis.

The simple white walls were accented by dark wooden beams in the low ceiling and the dark wood furniture placed around the room in an open fashion. Several chairs, a piano, a round table, and a fireplace with a clock and two candles on the plain mantel were among the few remaining "eyewitnesses" of the many conversations that had taken place in this unassuming room.

We stood while our guide told us of the Ten Booms' "open house" ministry. They spent their lives welcoming visitors to their table as well as taking in foster children and hosting children of missionaries.

Noelle caught my eye and gave me a nod when he mentioned the foster children.

"This open-home attitude continued even after the Nazi occupation. Corrie's father, Casper, emphasized to his four children, wife, and the three aunts who lived with them the importance of honoring God's chosen people," the tour guide said.

"Corrie and her sister Betsie did not marry," the guide went on to explain. "The two women lived here and were in their fifties on that fateful day: February 28, 1944. That was the day the family was betrayed to the Gestapo for assisting Jews as well as those in the underground resistance. The home was raided and the family taken to prison."

Our guide nodded toward a photograph of Casper, the patriarch of the family. "He was eighty-four years old when he was taken to Scheveningen Prison. When asked if he knew he could die for helping Jews, Casper replied, 'It would be an honor to give my life for God's ancient people.' He did in fact die only ten days after the arrest. Please, follow me now to the dining room."

We shuffled solemnly to a more compact room where it was explained that around this small dining table the nine members of the Ten Boom family gathered for daily Bible reading and prayer.

"This was a place of love and laughter, of prayer and ultimately of sacrifice. You will notice the open Bible on the table.

This is Casper's Bible. It is open to his favorite passage, Psalm 91. Does anyone here read Dutch?"

Noelle nodded.

"Would you care to read the first few verses of the psalm?" he asked.

Noelle stepped close to the table, and with her hands demurely folded in front of her, she read in Dutch.

The guide thanked her. He lifted a card from his pocket. "This passage in English might be familiar to some of you. Would you care to read it to us?" He was looking at me.

I took the card from him and read, "He who dwells in the secret place of the Most High shall abide under the shadow of the Almighty. I will say of the LORD, 'He is my refuge and my fortress; my God, in Him I will trust.'"

"Thank you." Our guide went on to explain that Corrie, after being the only family member to survive the Nazi death camp near Berlin, went on to spend the rest of her life traveling around the world and telling people about God's love.

"*Tante,* or aunt, Corrie, as those who loved her liked to call her, wrote a number of books, as you see in the case there on the wall. In 1975 a Hollywood film was released based on one of Corrie's books, *The Hiding Place.* Let us go single file now to Corrie's bedroom so you can see the actual hiding place."

Noelle and I lingered at the end of the group, examining the books in the case.

"I've read all her books," I said.

"You have?"

I nodded. "The first time I read one of her books was after my mother had gone to a church service where Corrie spoke. I finagled my way out of going, and my mother let me stay home. Whatever it was that Corrie said at that church service had a powerful effect on my mother. She always regretted not pressing me and our whole family to go.

"Several years ago when Wayne, the kids, and I watched the movie *The Hiding Place* at home, I told our children I almost had a chance to meet Corrie. They thought I meant during the war, as if I were that old." I chuckled to myself at the memory and added, "I do regret that I never got to meet her."

"You will." Noelle gave my shoulder a squeeze. "You'll meet her, and so will I. In heaven. We'll go together to her new home there. How would that be for a visit?"

At that moment, standing in the Ten Boom home, I had a tender flash, which is completely different from a hot flash. It was one of those heartwarming moments when heaven suddenly seems real. What follows is an unexpected calm, accompanied by a feeling of anticipation, or maybe it would be more accurate to call it a longing for home, as in heaven.

The truth at the center of that tender flash was the realization of how much there is to look forward to in eternity. I spend so much of my time focusing on what I can see and what I can control, yet real life—eternal life—is outside of time and beyond all limitations.

"You're right. I will get to meet her. We both will."

"It will be like a blink of time before we're all together," Noelle said. "That's how Jelle's mother talked about looking forward to heaven. She kissed all of us a few hours before she died, and then she said, 'See you in a minute.'"

Noelle and I caught up with the rest of the tour group. I thought about that concept—of stepping outside of time. Is that what it would be like to enter heaven? Would it be a mere blink of an eye from the moment a loved one crossed into eternity and when we join that person?

We followed single file down the narrowest hallway I had ever been in. Earlier we had been told Corrie's grandfather had built the house in 1837, which meant the building was already more than a hundred years old when World War II broke out. Everything was much closer quarters than I had pictured when I read Corrie's books and watched the movie.

Once we were assembled in the bedroom, we were shown the closet with the false wall at the back. We were told that on the day of the Gestapo raid, four Jews and two Dutch underground workers slipped through the sliding door at the back of the linen closet and crawled into the tight space behind the false wall.

Holding out his hand, our guide explained, "The wall here has been opened so you can see how much space was available for the six people who went into hiding here. They had only a few modest provisions, as you can see there, and a vent to the outside for fresh air. Even though the guards checked the house thoroughly, they didn't find the valuable human treasure hidden behind this wall. Those six people waited in silence for forty-seven hours after the raid until they were rescued by the underground. All six of them left this house safely."

I waited to be the last one in the group to look into the

cramped space and to try to imagine how those six people must have felt, waiting for deliverance. How did they do it? Two days without water, light, or any way to know if they would be found.

As I stepped forward and peered into the hiding place, my eyes filled with tears. How terrified those people must have been. Thoughts of fear, hate, and prejudice pressed against my chest.

I always had thought of myself as an open person when it came to ethnic diversity. Two of our daughters were from Korea, and both our foster sons were of African American descent. I didn't think I had a limited view of race.

However, the piercing and uncomfortable truth was that only an hour or so earlier I had been afraid of another human—a young Middle Eastern woman. Why? She was dressed like someone who lived in a part of the world I had come to think of as enemy territory. Her culture, religious background, and homeland might well have been on the list that my government and my cultural community would consider enemies.

So I was afraid of her. Yet she was only a frightened young woman. Frightened of me because I was an American. Did Noelle tell her I was just another woman? a friend? and above all, a Christian? That was the bond all of us had that went far beyond national and political lines of intolerance.

Our guide's steady voice ushered me back to the moment. "Many visitors to this room say they are glad such desperate occurrences are not happening in our world today. However, that is not true. Persecution continues. We might not be aware of where or how others are in a hiding place this very moment in another part of the world, but it is a fact."

The guide paused. I turned back to face the rest of our small group, aware that I too had prejudices.

The guide continued in the spirit of hope that had accompanied his summaries in each room so far. "Corrie was fifty-three when she was released from Ravensbrueck. This was shortly after her sister, Betsie, died in that same concentration camp. For the next thirty-three years Corrie traveled around the world repeating two truths she and her sister had learned while in prison. Do any of you know what those two themes were for Tante Corrie?"

The woman from South Africa spoke up in a soft voice. "There is no pit so deep that God's love is not deeper still."

The guide nodded. "Yes. That is the first. The other truth she taught was 'God will enable you to forgive your enemies.' "

The two women from Japan reservedly dipped their heads.

"I personally know this is true because my parents also died at Ravensbrueck. Their only crime was this: my parents were Jewish."

With his brow lowered he said, "I was four years old at the time they were taken. My mother managed to secretly entrust me to a Dutch family in the south. They were Catholic, and yet they took me in, kept me hidden until the war ended, and raised me as their own."

The room had gone very still. I drew in a breath of steadying air. All of this—the tour, the room, the horrors of the war— seemed true, intimate, and very personal as the guide continued with his story.

"I know that what Corrie believed is true. God will enable you to forgive your enemies because that has been my experience. As a young man, I met Corrie and heard her story. At the time I refused to open my heart to the same love that had given her such freedom. Many years later, after I married, my wife was given one of Corrie's books. I read it when no one was looking. I knew that anger and bitterness toward the Nazis had eaten holes in my life."

With a softening around his eyes, he concluded, "I asked God to enable me to forgive my enemies, and He did. That very day. I have not been the same since because, on that day, God also forgave me for my hatred and prejudice. He welcomed me into His family through His Son, the Messiah."

Noelle and I exchanged glances. I could tell she was as deeply touched by his personal account as I was.

"We celebrated Corrie's birthday earlier this week. She was born on April 15. She also passed away on April 15, on her ninety-first birthday. This is part of her story I feel honored to tell because, in the Jewish tradition, only those who are greatly blessed are allowed the special privilege of dying on their birthday."

I could have stayed in that room for a long time, just standing, thinking, and taking inventory of my feelings. I knew I needed time to sort out all the thoughts and images we had been presented. This was a place of simple serenity as well as betrayal and fear.

We then climbed to the very top of the house and entered a small room with a steeply slanted ceiling. For quite some time our small group lingered in the compact quarters, viewing an extensive display of family photos, plaques, and papers related to the house and to Corrie and her travels.

After reading a special poem written for Corrie, I looked at a photo taken of her during her traveling years. Viewing her image up close, I saw a woman whose unshakable love for God seemed to shine through every pore on her character-chiseled face. I wondered if my love for God was about to be shaken and tested.

What if I have cancer? How much time do I have left? What will happen once I return home? Why is this happening to me? Why now?

Noelle purchased several books and looked at me with my folded arms guarding all the mixed feelings in my stomach.

"You ready for some lunch?"

I followed her out into the alleyway even though the last thing I felt like doing at the moment was eating.

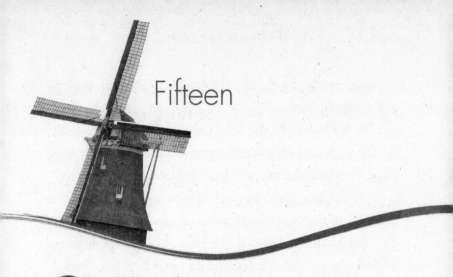

Fifteen

Once we were outside, Noelle suggested we walk to the market square about a block from the Ten Boom house. I followed as if in a trance.

Noelle stopped at the first café she came to. The menu was posted under glass by the restaurant's front door.

While Noelle skimmed the menu, I stood fixated on the massive, Gothic-style church in the far corner of the square. I never had seen such a large cathedral. It had to be several hundred years old and was majestic in its girth and structure.

"No." Noelle stepped away from the posted menu. "This is not what we want."

The sun had broken through the thin clouds, and dozens of bicyclists pedaled across the uneven, wide-open square. Several tables covered with bright yellow umbrellas lined up on one side of the church.

"What about over there?" I liked the idea of sitting down and reconnecting with my center of gravity, which had been thrown off balance.

"Sure, we can eat outside. The weather might even cooperate and not sprinkle on us."

We trekked across the open market square. In an effort to introduce a topic far from the thoughts that had taken me hostage, I said, "I wonder if Corrie and her family went to this church."

"It's not likely. Do you remember the guide saying they belonged to the Dutch Reformed denomination? This is Saint Bavo. It's a Catholic cathedral. If I remember correctly, this is one of the few in the region that escaped the iconoclastic riots. It might have been converted into a Protestant church. I don't remember the history."

I wasn't sure what she was talking about. I had no idea what an "iconoclastic riot" was.

"Have you been inside?"

"Yes, a long time ago. We came for an organ concert. Do you want to see if we can go inside? It's quite an organ, if you're familiar with church organs."

I wasn't. But it seemed like a good idea now that Noelle had suggested it. I hoped that walking and focusing on whatever we saw inside would release the cramping of feelings in my gut.

We entered the massive church, and the chill of the vast open space had a clarifying effect on me.

As our eyes adjusted to the shadowed interior, Noelle raised her chin up toward the sweepingly tall stained-glass windows. "Beautiful, aren't they?"

I nodded but didn't have the right words to respond. The interior was decorated ornately, yet it was the light exploding from the magnificent stained-glass windows that dominated the space. The high ceilings seemed a dizzying contrast to the compact, narrow hallways and rooms we had just been in at the Ten Boom house.

The organ, gilded with ornate carvings and intricate details, reigned over an entire section of the interior. Two larger-than-life statues were mounted atop protruding pillars on the face of the organ. I never had seen anything so grand. It looked like the front of a crown that would have fit on the head of a giant the size of a mountain. I couldn't quite grasp how extraordinary this instrument was. It was a work of art.

Noelle whispered to me, "That is the world's most famous organ facade. Mozart performed here, as did Haydn and Liszt, if I remember correctly. Impressive, isn't it?"

I nodded, feeling hushed and humbled by the sheer size of this place of worship.

"You should hear the music that comes out of that organ. It really is like nothing you've ever heard."

"You were saying something about riots. Was that during the war also?"

"No, the iconoclastic riots were five hundred years ago."

I tried to wrap my mind around this building being constructed more than half a millennium ago. It proved to be a challenging concept in light of how "old" everything had seemed at Corrie's house.

"I've never heard of these riots. What happened?"

Noelle directed me away from the pews where several people

were seated in quiet contemplation. We regrouped to the side of the church under one of the magnificent stained-glass windows. The early afternoon light was coming in through the windows and leaving pale stains of color on the floor and dark pews, bringing splashes of color, hope, and cheer into the church.

"This is what I know about the iconoclasts, but don't quote me on the accuracy of my facts. During the Reformation many— I guess you could say religious—people were focused on the importance of relics and icons."

"Such as crosses? Is that what you mean by an icon?"

"Yes and no. Some icons were paintings of Christ or the Nativity. Relics were bits of souvenirs brought back from the Crusades. Any sort of religious art might fall into the category of an icon, depending on your opinion of what were acceptable and unacceptable artistic expressions of worship. Does that make sense?"

I nodded, even though all this was new to me, and I wasn't completely up to speed.

"A movement rose up in Holland to destroy all the icons to purify the church. At the time, these items were symbols of Christianity, but some considered that the value placed on the pieces of art fell into the category of idol worship. Have you heard this before?"

"No, never. Keep going."

"Well-meaning, devoted believers came to cathedrals like this one and destroyed countless paintings, stained-glass windows, and especially carvings such as ornate wooden crosses or images of saints."

"That's why you were saying this church was spared."

"Right. I'm sure the whole story is included in the brochure they have at the entrance. We'll pick one up before we leave. Do you want to stay longer? We can walk around some more, if you like."

"No, I feel better. I mean, I'm ready to go. I could use something to eat, though."

"Me too."

I took a last look at the opulent beauty that surrounded me before we exited. The sunlight continued to press its soft rays through the colorful bits of glass in the windows. It would take hours, maybe days, to absorb all the details in the architecture and interior design of this spacious place. What a sharp contrast to the cramped quarters of the Hiding Place.

Five hundred years ago well-meaning purists rioted, and untold numbers of priceless pieces of art, carvings, and stained-glass windows were destroyed. But not these windows.

A generation ago a zealous dictator entered this same city on a much more serious "purification" rampage. We had heard on the Hiding Place tour that the Dutch lost around ten thousand soldiers and a hundred and ninety thousand civilians during World War II. However, due to the Ten Boom family not only hiding people but also being a distribution center for travel documents, an estimated eight hundred people were spared.

I felt a shiver of hope for the human race. God always seems to keep a certain remnant for Himself—from Noah's ark until the present. I wondered if I dared to reach for a shiver of hope for myself.

Noelle and I squinted as we stepped into the sunlight. We

settled into the chairs at one of the tables with the yellow umbrellas. Our lunch order was for two salads and a cup each of what Noelle translated as potato soup.

Noelle sat back. "This was a good choice to come here. Especially now that the weather is turning. The sun feels wonderful, doesn't it?"

I agreed and said I felt as if I could sit there for the rest of the day in silence and still barely process all that had happened since we left her house that morning.

"This has been quite a day, hasn't it? You know, I'm surprised I've lived here so long and yet never heard of the Ten Boom Museum. I'm going to tell everyone I know to visit the house. Everyone is aware of the Anne Frank house in Amsterdam. It's a fantastic museum, and the tour is thought provoking and moving. But of all the times I've gone there, I've never come away with a sense of hope riding on top of all the devastating emotions. I don't know if that is coming out the way I mean it. I felt something very deep at the Ten Boom house that went beyond the horrors of the Holocaust. Didn't you?"

"Yes, definitely."

Catching a hint of sadness or perhaps a brush of pain in Noelle's expression, I looked at her more closely. "What did you feel?"

"Too much."

I waited for her to elaborate.

"The part about forgiveness…about asking God to give you the strength to forgive someone…"

Her expression made it clear that something important yet delicate lay hidden in her life. I leaned forward, inviting her to tell me what it was.

Instead of opening up, she reached into her purse and put on a pair of sunglasses. All the heart messages that had been evident in her eyes were silenced. She had pulled down a shade, blocking my view. In a steady voice Noelle said, "I feel as if I need to just sit in the middle of all these thoughts and impressions for a while. I don't have conclusions yet."

"We can sit. Sitting is good."

Each of us drew in a slow breath, nearly in unison, and leaned back. I thought of all the years Noelle and I had experienced long stretches of silence. Sometimes she and I would go ten or more months without a single letter passing between us.

It didn't alter our friendship. We both seemed to know that when we sailed into a smooth-enough place in life, we could sit down and spill out our hearts' contents again. We were good at picking up wherever we had left off and taking our friendship on from there.

That deep-rooted history of security in the silences allowed us to sit across from each other in the sunshine and quietly dip our spoons into the thick potato soup without exchanging any words.

I missed Wayne. He was a truth teller. He would know what to say to Noelle right now. He would know how to nudge her to open up about whatever was causing her pain. Even I knew that it wasn't good to hold things inside for a long time. Truth always surfaces anyhow.

You're one to talk about opening up and speaking truth!

I brushed away the accusation. It was true, though. I was holding something delicate inside as well. Who was I to counsel Noelle to open up when I wasn't willing to do the same?

I thought of how Wayne had been okay with my leaving for this trip in a state of denial. If he knew what I was feeling about the possible cancer diagnosis, he would encourage me to express my thoughts to Noelle instead of holding them in.

I knew I could tell Noelle anything. She had been so accepting when I initially e-mailed her and said I was coming to see her. The only reason I gave her for this trip was that I had the time and needed to add a little spice to my flattened life since the kids had moved out. If she had suspected a deeper reason, she hadn't alluded to it in our conversations so far.

As I let a small bite of goat cheese from the salad linger on my tongue, I considered how I would bring up the topic of the biopsy. If I opened up to Noelle, perhaps she would feel free to open up to me.

But I didn't say anything.

I don't know why. Maybe because the day already seemed so intense. Or perhaps I was afraid that the lightness of our shared moments together would turn into a heaviness that would be difficult to get out from under once my dominating topic was in the open. Everything had been sailing along so smoothly. I didn't want to alter that.

We took our time over lunch. I decided I could take my time too with disclosing what was going on inside me. I could offer that same freedom to Noelle. We would take our time and see where our conversations naturally led. For now it was good just being "us" on this maiden voyage of the face-to-face season of our friendship.

To complete our sunny afternoon, Noelle and I walked to one of the main canals that connected Haarlem to Amsterdam. A variety of sailboats, motorboats, and even a few rowboats dotted the wide canal. On the other side of the water was an old house that had a windmill on top.

"This is so quaint. This is how I envisioned the Netherlands. It's like a picture book."

"You're definitely going to appreciate Amsterdam then. You know, we could still go there today, if you like. It's not far."

I hesitated.

"Or we could get a fresh start in the morning and spend all day there."

"I like that idea better."

Continuing at our leisurely pace, I took pictures of the boats, the canal, and the windmill while Noelle explained how Haarlem was a port city on the North Sea. The low, flat barges on the canals had been the main transportation source for many years until the arrival of the train.

"How far is the North Sea from here?"

"Close."

"Is it close enough that we could walk there?"

"Yes, we could do that. Would you like to go to the beach to see the North Sea?"

She said later that my eyes lit up like a child's when she asked if I wanted to go to the beach.

I told Noelle I wanted to put my toes into the North Sea. "I don't know why. It just seems like an exotic thing to be able to say that I did. 'I touched the North Sea.'"

"Whatever floats your boat," Noelle responded with a clever grin, as if she felt quite pleased with her on-the-spot pun.

I would have offered a courtesy grin back, but she already had taken off at her usual fast clip, and I was too busy breathing and trying to keep up with her to grin or utter a clever line in response.

Our direct route took us through some not-so-quaint parts of town and was a longer hike than I had expected. Walking seemed to invigorate Noelle and also seemed like a normal part of each day for her.

No wonder she's so fit and trim! I feel like a slug trying to keep up with her.

I remembered that she already had taken a long hike that morning when she walked to the car at the church parking area in The Hague. Once I caught my breath, I decided I would tell her how I thought The Hague was "the hag." She would get a laugh out of that.

But at the moment I wasn't laughing about anything. I was too breathless.

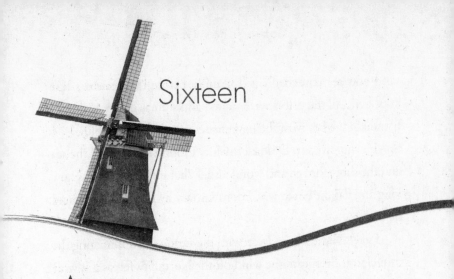

Sixteen

As Noelle and I entered the official beach area, we strolled past a number of cafés and bars that lined the walkway, facing the beach. If weather conditions were just right, I could see how this would be a popular spot in the summer.

"We ate at that café last autumn. It was a perfect day. Two of Jelle's cousins met us there with their families. The party got rowdy. Do you still use that word *rowdy?*"

I nodded.

"We were rowdy. Very loud. But then, I guess this is the place to come and be loud and have fun. We certainly had fun."

I noticed quite a few people were strolling up and down the walkway, bundled up and enjoying the brisk wind and the afternoon sunshine. Spring seemed to be in the air, and the locals were out experiencing a first taste of the sun, as we were.

Noelle stopped where the walkway met the sand. I put my hands on my hips and drew in long, deep breaths of the salty air. I had to admit this was pretty exhilarating. And beautiful. The sand and sea stretched out for miles before the horizon's line appeared. All the colors were muted and soft, as if they had been blended together with the base shades of pale gray and blue.

Having lived in Ohio all my life, I found the sight of the sea and the shore foreign and wonderful. What surprised me was how long and flat the beach was. I don't know why I imagined it would be rocky.

I gave a little shiver. Even with the steady sun dominating the thin clouds overhead, the wind off the North Sea felt as if it were whistling right through me. All the perspiration from our aerobic arrival was acting as a natural cooling system.

"Brrr!"

"Brisk, isn't it?"

I nodded.

"Do you still want to go down to the water?"

"Yes, definitely. I didn't come this far just to take a picture. I have to touch the water."

"Okay, if you insist. Right this way, Summer Breeze."

"Oh, don't I wish this breeze was a summer breeze!"

I don't think she heard my comment because she was trudging through the sand. She stopped at the shoreline.

"There you have it. The great North Sea. Are you sure you want to put your foot in?"

"I have to. I want to say I went to the North Sea and got in, even if it's only my pinkie toe that actually goes in."

"Go ahead. I have no desire to join you."

I removed only one shoe and sock instead of both. Hopping

through the cold, wet sand, I approached the water. The sea was calm, lapping the shore in small, rounded curls, as if it were a lake and not part of an ocean.

Overhead, a large sea gull swooped down and did a peglegged hop across the shore, approaching me like a beggar. His beady black eyes searched me for food.

"Sorry, no snacks for you today." I waved my shoe, expecting the bird to fly off elsewhere to plead his case.

The gull stayed and suddenly was joined by six companions. All of them pleaded for treats in a chorus of chortling cries.

"You've attracted an audience." Noelle held up her camera and captured the moment. "Go ahead. Dip your toe in the water. I'll take your picture."

I stepped closer to the water, ready to pose in ballerina fashion. The birds gathered in closer. "How do I tell them in Dutch to go away?"

Four more gulls had joined the gang. All of them moved toward me like a choreographed alley scene from *West Side Story*.

"They're going to attack me!"

Noelle laughed. "No they're not. Wave your shoe at them."

"I already tried that."

I waved my single, removed shoe in the air one more time and called out, "Shoo!" Only one bird moved, and his movement was barely a flinch.

Noelle cracked up. "You look like you're trying to teach them English, standing there with your shoe in the air and yelling 'shoe' to them."

"Very funny. I'm trying to make them go away. I was saying 'shoo' as in 'shoo—go away.'"

"Apparently they don't understand threats in English. You could always run toward them. I should think that would be interpreted as a universal gesture of aggression and should make them scatter."

I took off running, one shoe on my right foot, the left shoe in my hand, waving over my head. The ringleader started hopping back, opening his great white wings and squawking in protest.

I don't know if it was the imbalance of running in the sand with only one shoe on or the humbling fact that it had been many years since I had run so fast. Whatever the reason for my klutz moment, I tripped and did a colossal face-plant in the wet sand.

Boom.

Like a toppled statue, I fell just as the lapping waters curled toward the shore and clutched me with an icy embrace. I let out a wail—partly from the shocking sensation of the frigid water that had covered the entire left side of my body before receding to the depths and partly because that's the pitiful sound my pride makes when it's wounded.

Noelle was at my side immediately, pulling me up, rattling off all the expected concerned questions. Was I okay? Did I need help getting up? Was I hurt anywhere?

Once I was vertical and it was clear nothing was broken, I could see in the corners of her eyes a burst of laughter dying to come out and play.

Wiping the wet sand from the side of my mouth and releasing an involuntary shiver, I kept a straight face as if nothing out of the ordinary had happened. In my best deadpan voice I said, "That oughtta frighten those birds. It certainly scared the life outta me."

Noelle's giggle gave way to a full burst of laughter as I limped in an exaggerated way and went ka-lumping down the shore in an attempt to retrieve my shoe and sock. The wayward pair had turned into a bird-seeking missile during my fumbling fall. The sock-loaded shoe had missed its unintended target in the launch and landed in the sand. Now the icy fingers of the North Sea curled around my shoe, beckoning it to come with them into the abyss. My shoe tipped to its side, as if listening to the call of the deep, but the wise ol' sole hesitated to accept the invitation to go for a dunk.

I quickened my pace toward my shoe, but the gulls, with the advantage of their wings, arrived at the shoe before I did.

The resilient Dutch feathered resistance had been unruffled by my charge-and-topple attack. There they were, back on the scene, boldly launching an in-depth investigation. Their curious, long sea gull bills were poking and prodding every corner of my shoe.

"Leave it alone! Shoo! Shoo from my shoe, you shoosters!"

The ringleader with the peglegged hop managed to firmly grasp my sock. He extracted it from the shoe and held it like a dead fish, drooping lifeless in his beak.

"Hey, drop it!" I waved my hands and made an aggressive yet wisely nonsprinting movement toward him.

The gull flapped his wings. His cohorts did the same. They seemed to loudly protest his greed. Two of them pecked at my sock from the side, trying to extract the treasure from his grasp.

"It's a sock!" I hollered at the birds. "You can't eat it! Drop it! Hey, stop! No, don't you dare!"

With a flip of his feathered behind, the sea gull spread his wings and took off over the North Sea with all his gang members launching into flight right behind him. My sock, still clamped in his mouth, was the prize of the day.

"Are you kidding me?"

The taunting thief was about two hundred feet out over the North Sea, flying low, when he apparently realized the nonexistent nutritional value of my fuzzy footwear. As Noelle and I watched, the sea gull dropped my sock into the sea.

Noelle laughed before I did. She wrapped both her arms around my shoulders and let loose with the sort of rollicking belly laugh I always knew she was capable of delivering.

We stood on the shore, with Noelle laughing her heart out and me saying, "I'm sure this will be a lot funnier to me at a later time, but right now I really am in desperate need of a rest room."

With my sockless, numb, sand-covered foot thrust inside my soggy shoe, I shuffled alongside Noelle to the nearest café that would let us use their rest room.

I couldn't clean up properly. The entire left side of my body was soaked with seawater and sprinkled with sand. A small piece of something oceanic and strange had latched on to my hair. It had the texture of green moss growing on a piece of dirty plastic.

With the indulgence of way too many paper towels, I did my best to become publicly presentable. My efforts deserved a grade of about a C-.

Noelle was patient. I appreciated that she was a compassionate woman. That quality had been obvious when she jumped in to assist Zahida that morning.

In her generous effort to help me, she arranged for a taxi to drive us back to the parking garage. I was grateful I didn't have to walk all the way back with one shoe leaving a salty footprint everywhere I placed my foot.

Once we were settled in little Bluebell, I think Noelle and I exhausted just about every bird, shoe, klutz, and sock joke we could think of on our uncomfortable ride home. The discomfort for me was from the cold. The discomfort for Noelle was that she kept the heater running at full speed to help me dry while she perspired in the salty sauna conditions.

She told me about a summer when they tried to take a picnic to the beach and a rainstorm had ruined the day. They drove home that time with the heater running the whole way and the scent of sea brine filling the car.

"Everyone was so grouchy. We sat in traffic for a horribly long time because it was one of the finals before the European Cup, and we had won. Everyone was more interested in cheering and celebrating than in keeping the cars moving."

"Forgive my ignorance, but what is the European Cup?"

"Football. Or I guess I should call it soccer since that's what you call it in the U.S."

"I have heard that soccer is a big deal here."

"You have no idea. You should come back with Wayne and visit sometime during the World Cup. Everyone wears orange, our national color, to show support. As a nation of more than sixteen million people, we do a good job of rallying around our team."

"Did you say sixteen million?"

Noelle nodded.

I tried to picture that many people fitting into the small landmass that comprised the Netherlands. No wonder the houses were built up instead of out and were so close together.

"I had no idea so many people lived here. I was looking at a map on the plane and saw that the country isn't that big."

"No, it's not. And if you want to really be impressed, I'll tell you that we are third in the world for agricultural exports. The U.S. is first, then France, then the Netherlands. How's that for a country with a fraction of the landmass of the others? I think it's a third of the country that is below."

"Below what?"

"Below sea level. Engineers continue to find ways to dredge land from the sea. That's how the usable landmass keeps growing."

"Well, one of these days they'll scoop up land from the bottom of the sea, and my sock will be there, mixed in with all the sand and silt."

Noelle laughed. "A little part of you will forever be a part of the Netherlands. I love it!" We rode for a few minutes, both smiling.

"Noelle, do you ever miss home?" I had noticed the way she aligned herself with the surrounding culture yet at the same time talked about being appreciative of having me, another American, visit her.

"This is my home," she said firmly. "I have lived here twice as long as I lived in the U.S. I love it here. Hup Holland!" The last line came out strong like a cheer.

"What was that?"

"The national cheer for our football team. I told you, we're passionate about our team. By the way, can you feel your toes yet?"

"Just barely. Are you melting? You may turn off the heater, if you like."

In her best *Wizard of Oz* witch voice, she said, "I'm melt-ing!"

As she turned down the heat, we launched into a fun discussion of how we both were terrified of the flying monkeys in that movie. Then we disclosed our *Sound of Music* desire to be Julie Andrews when we were twelve so we could become nannies and skip through Austria with our own entourage of adoring adolescents wearing lederhosen.

The conversation helped speed up the ride back to Noelle's. The first thing I did on arriving was to shake off the dried sand before I went into the house. The same neighbor who had heard me call Noelle an oen took a moment to observe me slapping my jeans—only the left side, mind you—and hopping and shaking to get the sand off.

I was almost adjusting to the reality that the neighbors could observe so much of what I did while at Noelle's.

A long bath was next on the list for this unusual day. This was definitely a private event. The bath was great. Relaxing and restorative. The kind of leisurely bath I never allowed myself to take the time to enjoy at home.

After I returned to the guest room in my robe, feeling all steamy and fresh scented with my clean hair wrapped in a towel, I found a tray waiting for me with a note from Noelle. She had fixed a sandwich along with a glass of milk. Her note said that Jelle had called and needed her to pick him up at work. I had forgotten that they shared one car, which was possible due to the convenient public transportation.

She went on to write that the two of them would stop on the way home for dinner since she assumed I planned to go to bed early.

The end of her note read: "If this sandwich doesn't interest you, please help yourself to anything you would like. My refrigerator is your refrigerator. Except I'm sure mine is emptier and doesn't yet have as many cool photos on it as yours does. But I'm working on that and feel confident that my current exhibit will be a crowd pleaser."

I took the bait from her teasing last line and made a little trip downstairs. It felt odd being the only one in the house, tiptoeing around in my p.j.'s.

A light was on over the kitchen sink. It illuminated the room enough for me to easily view Noelle's spur-of-the-moment photo addition to the front of her refrigerator.

I stood there, barefoot, in Noelle's kitchen, laughing until my sides hurt. She had printed out a picture in black and white on a basic sheet of computer paper. Obviously she had done it as a joke. And what a joke it was. The shot was of me at the shoreline attempting to chase the birds. My arms were in the air, and in front of me, as clear as could be, was the pesky sea gull clutching my sock and spreading his wings.

She had captured the moment perfectly.

While the whole fiasco was happening, I was so caught up in trying to get the bird to stop that I hadn't seen much humor in it. I was desperate to retrieve my sock and not objective enough to realize how funny the scene must have looked to Noelle.

Now, even in black and white, I could see what a frolic it was and why Noelle had let loose with a belly laugh.

I lingered in the kitchen, helping myself to a handful of grapes from the bowl of fresh-washed and still-glistening beauties Noelle had left on the counter. I wanted to remember this. The laughter, the friendship, the comfort. The peace. This gentle longing for "home."

As the deep purple grape burst open in my mouth and filled my senses with the rich taste of communion, I felt as if I were closing the day by savoring a little taste of heaven.

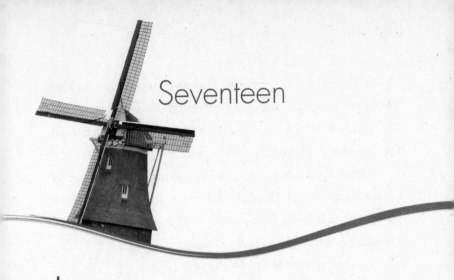

Seventeen

I started the next day with morning devotions again. I was glad Noelle had left the book by my bed. I hadn't packed my Bible, and to be honest, in the past few months I had been inconsistent in doing any daily Scripture reading. My soul felt hungry and ready for each word.

The devotional for that day was entitled "Even Though I Walk." The passage from the Bible that started off the reading was Psalm 23. I read it quickly, feeling familiar with the passage. Then I remembered how I had felt like a little lost sheep the day before as I drove Noelle's car to the church parking lot. I didn't enjoy that feeling, but this morning, secure in the warm guest bed, I realized I was more open and vulnerable to God as a result of driving around directionless. In fact, this new day I wanted God to be my Shepherd.

A few hours later, walking with Noelle to the train station for our journey to Amsterdam, I thanked her for putting the devotional by my bed. I told her how much I was enjoying it and commented that the reading for the day was from Psalm 23.

"The title of the entry seems pretty fitting for us, the way we've been walking all over the Netherlands since I arrived."

"I hope it hasn't been too much walking for you. Jelle needed the car today. And the train station isn't far."

"I don't mind. I'm just not used to walking so much. It's good for me." I moved my shoulder bag to my other arm. "So, even though we walk to the train station, I will fear no evil. Or maybe I should say, I will fear no muscle cramps."

"Or maniacal sea gulls," Noelle added.

"That's what I should have been praying yesterday. 'Even though I walk through the valley of the shadow of sea gulls…'"

Noelle turned to me with a light-bulb-over-the-head sort of expression.

"What?"

"I never noticed that part before. 'Even though I walk through the valley of the shadow of death.'"

"What part had you not noticed?"

"The verse says even though we 'walk' through the valley. That's different from stopping in the valley or sitting down under the shadow of death and just giving up. We aren't supposed to stop and get stuck in the dark places. We're to keep going. Keep walking. I really like that thought, don't you?"

I nodded, holding in the depth of my truer feelings. Noelle had no idea how poignant her insights were to me at that moment. The threat of cancer was my valley of the shadow of death. I had involuntarily taken the first step into that valley the day I answered the phone call from my doctor's assistant.

Here I was, in the valley of the shadow of death. Was I fearing no evil? God was with me. His rod and staff were there to comfort me. What represented His rod and staff in my life?

I pictured Noelle and Wayne as being two very effective tools in the hand of the Great Shepherd. God was using both of them to keep me close to Him, which is what I always pictured as the purpose of a rod and staff. Wasn't the rod used for discipline and the staff used to rescue?

Once again, just as I had sensed while waiting for Noelle in the church parking lot yesterday, I saw myself as God's little lamb. I was more helpless than I wanted to admit, but I also was being cared for more deliberately and tenderly in this valley than I would have guessed possible. I was loved. What a great gift that was.

"Thank you, Noelle." Tilting my head to offer her an appreciative grin, I tried to impress her by saying it in Dutch. *"Bedankt."*

"You're welcome. But what are you thanking me for?"

"For walking with me."

"Okay…"

I didn't want to add the part about walking through the valley of the shadow of death, although, at the moment, talking about it didn't feel as monstrously frightening as it had before. Still, I skirted the real thoughts that had prompted my thank-you.

"I appreciate your putting everything in your world on pause this week to give your time to me. You were very kind to let me show up the way I did and hijack your life."

"Are you kidding? Your visit has been such a lift for me. I was telling Jelle last night what a gift this is to me. I couldn't stop talking about the Ten Boom house while he and I were having dinner. He's never been there either. I'm taking him and the girls. And I'm reading all her books. Your visit is stirring up things in me that I walked away from a long time ago, and I don't know how I feel about all that yet. But I do know I need to pay attention to the feelings."

Our conversation would have gone further, but we were at the train station and had to hurry to make the train that was boarding just as we arrived.

We sat with mostly businesspeople. Our seats faced each other, and the view out the window was more expansive than what I had seen from the main roads. A uniformed conductor came down the aisle, asking for our tickets. We showed him the passes Noelle had arranged for earlier, before we dashed to board the train.

"Would you like a morning cup of hot chocolate?" Noelle stood up with her wallet in her hand. "This train has a beverage car."

"Sure. Should I come with you?"

"No, I'll be right back."

For breakfast I finally had tried the drinkable yogurt Noelle had purchased for me at the grocery store earlier in the week. It wasn't my favorite jump-starter beverage. Perhaps it was the texture and slightly sharp taste of the chocolate yogurt. The drink didn't go down smoothly.

I had higher hopes for the cup of Dutch chocolate Noelle handed to me a few minutes later. "That was fast."

"I was first in line. Doesn't happen often. Let me know how you like it."

I lifted my cup to hers. In a dull, barely audible tap of the cardboard rims, we toasted. "To a day without sea gulls," I said.

"To walking right on out of the valley of the shadow."

Instead of saying the customary "Cheers," we both said, "Amen." I took a sip and wondered what Noelle's valley was.

I would have pondered that thought more extensively, but my mind was diverted by the sensation of deep, rich chocolate rolling over my taste buds. Nary a bud was disappointed in the immersion. "Oh, this is good."

"You like it?"

"Most definitely. It seems to be more bittersweet than what I'm used to. Not that I'm a hot cocoa connoisseur. I love it. Does it have less sugar? Is that it?"

"I don't know. I think it has less alkaline or acid or something. I'll have to ask Jelle's sister. She's the Dutch chocolate expert. All I know is that it's processed differently than anywhere else in the world, and I happen to think it's the best."

"I would agree with you on that." I took another slow, savoring sip of the delectable Dutch chocolate from my cardboard to-go cup and gazed out the window. The train pulled into a stop at a town called Leiden, according to the sign on the landing.

More travelers boarded the train, filling the remaining empty seats. We hadn't gone far after that when the scene outside the train car window turned into what seemed like a wide, flat-screen view of a travel show that was better than anything I ever had watched at home.

We were passing a tulip field.

I held my breath as if I could hold in the sight of the flowers' color, symmetry, and brightness.

After the train rolled past the last row of dazzling tulips, I took another long sip of my Dutch chocolate and slowly turned to Noelle with a contented smile on my lips.

With a softening expression around her eyes, she leaned over and whispered, "You have a mustache."

I licked my upper lip and used the tip of my finger to finish the quick chocolate "shave." "Better?"

She nodded.

"Why don't you come to the States sometime?" I hadn't premeditated my question. It just jumped out, so I went with it. "You should come and bring Jelle. I would love it if you would stay with us. I'll show you all the sights. Of course, that will take about twenty whole minutes, but it would be fun. I really want Wayne to meet both of you."

Noelle smiled. "I'll have to think about that. Thank you for the invitation, Summer."

"I'll have lots of tortilla chips and salsa. Isn't that the food you once said you missed the most?"

"Yes. I don't think I've tasted a true Southwest tortilla chip or cilantro-laced salsa since I've lived here. Not like my mom used to serve."

"What else do you miss about the U.S.?"

"Candy."

I laughed. "Don't you have candy here?"

"We have lots of candy. Very good candy, just like our Dutch chocolate is very good. But when the girls were little, I wanted to buy kiddy candy for them like we grew up on at home. Here, it's not the same."

"No candy necklaces?"

"No. My girls grew up with a salty sort of licorice called *dropje.* I don't like it. Do you remember the pink bubblegum that came in little wrapped squares with cartoons folded up inside?"

"I loved that Bazooka bubblegum."

"And Neccos. Is that what they were called? The round, thin, wafer candies that came in a wrapped cylinder. I used to buy those when we went to the movies and let them sit on my tongue until they melted. My goal was never to chew them but just let them dissolve, one after the other. Same with Junior Mints. Do they still make Junior Mints?"

"Yes. Can I lure you to my corner of the world if I promise an unending supply of fresh salsa, Junior Mints, Bazooka bubblegum, and Neccos?"

"Your powers of persuasion are impressive."

The train rolled into a huge covered station. Noelle motioned that we should head for the front of our train car to exit now that the train had stopped. My powers of persuasion were apparently not impressive enough to convince her to continue the conversation.

As soon as we stepped off the train, I was awed by the enormity and detailed beauty of the station. Haarlem had seemed charming and Old-World. Amsterdam, starting with the train station, felt like an elaborate scene from an epic movie. I was only a walk-on character in the enchanting saga, but "walk" seemed to be the theme of the day, so on I walked.

Noelle had a map with her, which she pulled out as soon as

we exited the train terminal. "My recommendation is that we start with the Van Gogh. Is that okay with you?"

"Sounds good. Lead the way."

"We're going to take bikes. My girls say the best place to rent is this way." Noelle led me to an unassuming storefront. We entered, and there on the floor, stacked up on the walls, and hanging from the ceiling were bicycles. Every sort of bike imaginable was lined up, ready for rent. The orderly sections reminded me of the tulip fields, only without the color, fluidity, or grace. This field was a lot of metal, rubber, and spokes.

"Ready?" Noelle asked as soon as we had signed for our bikes and were on them. "Stay with me. We cannot get separated. If we do, ask anyone where the Rijksmuseum is, and go there."

"Rikes," I repeated. "'Rikes' like 'bikes.'"

"Yes. That museum is near the Van Gogh Museum. Anyone in Amsterdam should be able to tell you how to get there."

I had not been on a bicycle since... I couldn't remember when. I soon discovered that the saying about never forgetting how to ride is only partly true. I still remembered how to ride a bike, and once I was on, the pedaling part was automatic. What didn't come back naturally was remembering how to start. Do you sit down and balance yourself first before pedaling? Or do you stand to pedal?

My choice was to stay standing, just so I would have my feet ready to do the inevitable balancing. After two false starts, I was off. I'm not sure how. It seemed to be a combination of the standing, pushing off, then sitting and pedaling all at once that proved successful.

Noelle pedaled slowly. I appreciated that. We turned a corner, and suddenly we were engulfed in a torrent of bicyclists. I felt like a fish entering some sort of stream in the middle of a feeding frenzy. The grand swirl of bicyclists moved as one, turning another corner and picking up the pace.

We were apparently in rush-hour traffic in a lane on the main road that was designated for bikes only. What amazed me was how quiet it was for such a huge city. A tram packed with commuters glided along rails. Cheery bicycle bells rang as bicyclists alerted pedestrians of their impending turns. In bunches, cyclists would leave the pack and take off down side roads while a steady stream of new cyclists joined the pack.

I was exhilarated by the experience. Few people wore helmets or protective gear. The exception seemed to be the children in tow on the front or back of bikes steered by experienced parents. One man in a suit expertly balanced a young boy on the front of the bike and pedaled with a folding stroller strapped over his arm. I saw a striking blonde in a straight skirt and beautiful white blouse and fashionable sunglasses pedaling right along with a briefcase in a front basket and a helmet-wearing toddler in the seat behind.

I managed to stay beside Noelle in the swirl of morning movement. That in and of itself was miraculous, given the number of bicyclists that surrounded us.

"This way," Noelle called out to me. "Edge your way to the right."

I edged over. We turned down a wide street that soon became narrower. Another turn brought us upon one of the loveliest sights I had seen in any city anywhere.

We stopped and caught our breath, taking in the surroundings. A calm canal ran down the center of our view. Small boats floated in the canal, tethered to a variety of moorings. On either side of the canal ran a narrow space for parking. Every inch was taken by small vehicles jockeyed into position. Next to the parking was the narrow canal road, just wide enough for the likes of Bluebell to slide down. A sprinkling of bicyclists made their way up and down the canal road.

Beyond the road the houses rose proud and steady, like a gathering of inseparable sisters, attached at the hip, the ankle, the shoulder, the temple. Together they were immovable, and they were stunning with their rosy brick faces catching the morning light. They sat right on the road's edge, their windows open to the world.

Many of the steady sister houses rose with a single window on each floor. I counted six floors in one of the houses, and she was shorter than her adjacent sister.

The trees were the other piece of art in this still-life scene. These were old trees. Their trunks were dark and haggard looking, with all kinds of bumps and warts. But their limbs stretched out nimbly over the canal on one side and the narrow road on the other. From their branches sprouted vibrant new green leaves. Several trees down the canal were dressed up in pale pink blossoms. Why welcome spring in expected green when you can frill yourself up with party pink?

"Nice, isn't it?"

"It's gorgeous, Noelle. I'd like to take a few pictures."

"I thought you might. That's why we took this detour. Lean this way. Can you see the bridge there down the canal?"

Feeling the artistic inspiration of the moment, I pulled out my camera and handed it to Noelle. "Can you get me with the bike and the bridge in the back?"

"Sure, let's try."

I walked the bike through the sliver of space between the parked car next to us and the determined tree. The idea was to take a shot of me, not on the bike, but just with the bike, standing there with all the wonders of the light and colors of the canal providing the impressionistic background to the photo.

Anchoring the kickstand, I asked again, "Can you get the bridge in the background?"

"I think so. If you move a little more to your left..." Noelle looked at me over the top of the camera. "I'm kidding, you know."

Of course I knew. If I moved any more to the left, I would be on my way into the canal. "Very funny."

"No, not very funny. I don't think you would enjoy one bit going for a swim in that canal water."

"I did my water aerobics in the North Sea yesterday." I maintained my grinning expression. I leaned against the anchored bike, head tilted just right. "I'm ready. Can you get the shot?"

"Yes. That's perfect. Hold still. Ready? One, two..."

Before Noelle said "three," a motor started up on a boat down the canal, startling me.

"Don't move! You have to stay right where you are. One, two, three." She took the shot.

I struck another pose and could hear the boat puttering in our direction.

Noelle lowered the camera and looked beyond me at the approaching boat. "Oh, Summer, you are not going to believe this! Don't move!"

She took several quick snaps before looking up at me again. I could tell that the boat was right behind me.

"Look," she said. "You would think I planned this."

I turned to see a boat in the shape of a giant wooden shoe motoring down the canal.

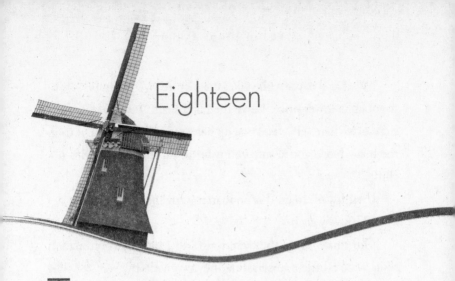

Eighteen

The cheery captain of the larger-than-life-sized, painted, wooden-shoe boat tipped his cap.

"Ask him if we can take a picture inside his boat."

Noelle gave me a skeptical look.

"I'm serious. Please ask him. I would love to have a picture of me sitting in that wooden shoe."

Noelle called out to him in Dutch, and the two of them entered into a short conversation. The captain steered the shoe, or rather the boat, to an open mooring at the edge of the canal near where we stood.

"He agreed?"

"Yes. He said he goes to the main tourist spots on the canals and takes pictures of children inside his shoe boat. He doesn't usually take adults, but this time he will make an exception. For a fee, of course."

My smile widened. I didn't care how much he charged. This was too perfect!

"I'll pay." I reached into my purse.

"Wait and pay after he takes the picture. We might be able to negotiate a lower price. Leave the bikes here. We'll go down the steps over there. He will come up here and take a picture of us in the boat. Now, you're sure you want to do this, because it's not cheap."

"Yes. I want to do this no matter what the price."

"This way then."

Our descent into the canal wasn't difficult. My coordination skills were a little embarrassing, but we made the transfer. The boat was so cute. It was about the size of a large rowboat but appeared to be crafted out of wood, just like a wooden shoe. It was painted a sunny yellow with tulips in red and green painted all around the outside.

The good-humored captain took his time finding just the right position at the top of the canal. Noelle and I got our balance inside the small boat. We set up the pose with our arms around each other.

"Sisterchicks in a wooden shoe!" I called out, feeling positively giddy.

Noelle chuckled. "You really are enjoying this, aren't you?"

"Yes! I think it's hilarious. Am I embarrassing you?"

"A little."

"A little, but not too much, right?"

Noelle paused.

"Is it too much of a touristy thing for you?"

"Yes, but who cares? It doesn't matter. You're right. This is good fun."

"Hey, if your husband and his cousins can sit around at an outdoor beach café, like you were telling me yesterday, and be loud and rowdy in public, then you and I can have some silliness in a wooden shoe on an Amsterdam canal."

"You're right."

"Besides, aside from you or me, who will ever know we did this?"

Noelle gave a mischievous chuckle. "That all depends on whether the photo makes it to my refrigerator gallery."

"Oh yes. I meant to comment on yesterday's art selection."

My echoing chuckle in the canal was followed by a strange and awful sound of metal falling on metal.

Noelle and I looked up just in time to see both of our bikes, untouched by human hands, falling one on the other and tumbling in an entwined, contorted swan dive into the canal.

"No!" we both screamed at the same moment.

The sound of the splash was disturbing on oh-so-many levels. The captain laughed erratically as he held up one of the cameras and shouted in English, "I took a photo!"

Stunned, I stepped back. As I did, my hip pressed against a button. I still don't know what it was or how it happened, but somehow I had started the engine. The wooden shoe began putt-puttering down the canal.

The man yelled at us in Dutch. Noelle reached for a lever on the handcrafted control panel. She flipped it up, but the motor kept going, and so did we, straight toward our submerged bikes.

The man yelled louder. Noelle called back something in

Dutch. He answered, and she tried another switch. The motor died, but we were now in the slow-moving current of the canal, drifting away from where we had entered.

"Weren't we roped to anything?" I steadied myself and kept an eye on the bikes as they slowly *glub-glub* sank into the canal.

"Apparently not. He said to sit. The boat tips easily."

I immediately sat. What I sat on, I'm not sure. Noelle sat on the boat's edge, opposite me. The owner of the runaway wooden shoe trotted along the canal, between the trees and parked cars, calling out orders. Several people in the previously quiet neighborhood stepped out onto the canal road to see what was going on.

"What do we do?" I asked.

"He says to stay balanced, and when we come to the turn, the canal narrows. We should try to find a way to pull to the side."

"How?"

"I have no idea."

To our right we passed the barely visible handlebars of our bikes. Fortunately, we hadn't left anything strapped to them. The unhappy rental bikes went to their watery grave alone.

"Keep a watch for any sort of rope or pole," Noelle said.

No rescue devices were to be seen. We weren't going fast. The problem was the tipsy nature of the unusually shaped craft and our inability to direct the way we were headed.

The closer we floated toward the more-populated area, the more attention we drew. The harried captain had disappeared since he couldn't round the corner of the canal by running alongside. He appeared on the other side of the turn, yelling at us, apparently for not managing to grab hold of anything in the narrows.

We were in a more-open, exposed part of the canal now. People stopped to stare. Children pointed. I heard loud exclamations of how cute we were from a huddle of college-aged girls. They were bent over a map until one of them caught sight of us. All of them pulled out their cameras and took our picture. I waved.

"What are you doing?" Noelle's words came out in a squawk.

"I'm waving."

"Why?"

"I don't know." I laughed. After yesterday's encounter with the gulls at the North Sea and the way I had missed all the humor in the moment, I felt the best response to this out-of-control situation was to sit back and enjoy the ride.

My sit-back-and-wave reaction was so out of the ordinary for neurotic little me that all I could think about was how proud my husband would be of me at this moment. I was so deep in denial that I was having fun.

Noelle covered her face with her hands and shook her head.

We were floating through Amsterdam as if it were the Wooden Shoe Day Parade and she and I were the lead float, so to speak. Before this day was over, someone somewhere would be checking a friend's blog to see how her visit to Amsterdam was going, and there would be a photo of Noelle and me, adrift in an oversized wooden shoe.

This was our fifteen seconds of fame.

I thought it was the funniest thing that had ever happened to me.

I waved again.

Just then, from overhead a long rope dropped down to us.

We were floating under an arched pedestrian walkway. The captain was yelling. Another man was with him, and they were holding fast to the other end of the rope.

I felt as if we were a pair of curious little monkeys and the man in the big yellow hat was trying to get us out of trouble.

Noelle sprang into action, reaching for the lowered rope. She planted her feet as the boat wobbled. The captain continued his directions. Noelle held on bravely, as we were pulled to the side of the canal.

I waved to a young couple with a baby. They waved back. The father lifted the baby's hand and had the baby wave back. I was having a lovely time.

The man with the rope hurried down the footbridge and somehow anchored the rope, then pulled us to shore with his brawny arms.

Our audience had swelled. We must have had close to a hundred people watch as Noelle and I tried to help each other scale a rickety metal ladder that was bolted into the brick side of the canal. My grip was so wobbly that kind and concerned Noelle had to give my behind a two-handed push of support to keep me moving up the ladder.

I tried hard not to laugh.

We managed to arrive unscathed atop the canal. One shop owner who stood in his doorway a few feet from us gave a friendly cheer. The rest of our audience stood and stared.

Seeing the gathered crowd, our skipper regained his merry disposition and called out to any and all takers, "Photos?"

At least twenty tourists congregated, holding out their cameras. Noelle and I sheepishly moved to the front of the line to retrieve our cameras. That is, if he hadn't tossed them into the canal when he took off chasing us. He handed us our cameras, I paid him the agreed-upon amount, and we all shook hands.

Walking away, Noelle said, "I think we just launched him from the kiddy boat business to a slightly more daring clientele."

"That was hilarious." I was still smiling. "What do you want to do now, Gilligan?"

"Gilligan?"

"Don't you remember *Gilligan's Island*?" I sang the theme song from the sitcom for her.

"The professor and Mary Ann. I forgot all about *Gilligan's Island*." Noelle still looked distracted. "As far as what we should do next, I don't know. Maybe report the bikes to the rental company?"

"I forgot about the bikes."

"You really did clock out of reality for a bit there, didn't you?"

Noelle walked and I followed. We boarded the tram and stood in the crowded space for several blocks, retracing the path we had taken earlier on the bikes. I was still grinning.

When we reported what had happened, the bike-rental manager appeared to be less affected than I thought he would be.

Noelle translated for me while he went for the papers for us to sign. "He said this happens more than you would think. It's usually cars that go in the canal. At least once a week. Someone forgets to set the parking brake, or they come home drunk. With no railing what can you do? Into the canal you go."

I was surprised to hear that cars plunged into the canal. Then I found out how much we would have to pay for our accident, and I was bummed. Noelle insisted we split the fee.

"It was no one's fault. They just fell in together. If anything, it was my fault because I should have thought to have you move your bike closer to mine by the road rather than for me to move mine over and rest it on yours."

All told, it took us about two and a half hours to get on with our day. Instead of renting any more bikes, we opted for tram passes and lots of walking.

First stop was still the Van Gogh Museum. The modern building looked like a big gray box. We had to wait in line to get in, and when we did, the lines were long as we wound through a display of the progression of the artist's work.

I spent the most time examining one of his famous sunflower paintings. In some places on the canvas, the paint was so thick it peaked like crests of orange and yellow waves. In other places, no paint had been applied at all, and the fine, woven texture of the canvas showed through.

His work showed his uniquely vibrant use of colors and the way he aggressively bent the perspective with his curved lines. The background information on his struggle with mental illness and his sense of failure really got to me. This brilliant artist created hundreds of works, yet only sold one piece in his lifetime.

When we reached the portion of the exhibit that represented the era of his life when he mutilated and cut off part of his earlobe, I felt deeply sad for him. I wasn't sure I wanted to finish walking through the display. I knew he took his own life. The final pieces he painted demonstrated a depth of depression and pain beyond anything I could imagine.

We left the museum quiet and somber.

Noelle suggested we find a place to eat before we attempted to appreciate the works of Rembrandt and Vermeer at the Rijksmuseum. That proved to be good advice because the expressions of art we viewed next were mind-boggling. Particularly the enormous *Night Watch* by Rembrandt. The painting took up an entire wall. The perfection of balance and color, contrast and light, made it feel as if the subjects could walk right off the canvas in their seventeenth-century garb.

We meandered our way into the next exhibit room, and I whispered to Noelle, "I had no idea this would be so overwhelming."

"What is overwhelming to you?"

"The art. All these masterpieces. I'm such a novice. Everything is brand-new to me. I mean, I recognized the Van Gogh sunflowers painting, but I don't know anything about Rembrandt or these other artists."

"You know about Vermeer. We haven't gone to the display of his work yet. You said you still had the postcard I sent you of his painting the *Kitchen Maid*. Or I guess, according to this brochure, the correct name for that painting is *The Milkmaid*."

"What I'm trying to say is that I don't feel as if I'm appreciating all of this sufficiently."

Noelle's expression softened. "Appreciation of beauty isn't work. All you have to do is look. Open your eyes, your mind, your heart. Take in whatever it is you see. Let the painting do all the work. Just listen with your eyes, and the painting will tell you its story."

I nodded, ready to try that approach. It could have been that, in my insecurity over my inexperience with such great works of art, I felt the need to form an opinion or to evaluate everything I was looking at. My shoulders relaxed. I was an observer, not a critic.

We slowly moved around the next room, looking at a number of portraits Rembrandt had painted. Each canvas captured the life of a person who lived hundreds of years ago.

One painting was of a woman with a round, cherubic face and tiny brown eyes like two buttons. The more I looked into those brown eyes, the more I wondered about who she was and what had happened during her life. How did she die?

Then, when I observed the rise in her cheekbones and the soft glow of her hair, the moist touch of health on her lips, I thought the better question to ask was, how did she live?

For a fraction of a blink, it seemed as if the woman in the painting had raised her eyebrow slightly and was asking the same question of me. Not how was I going to die, but how was I going to live?

"Fully," I answered in my head and in a whisper.

Nineteen

S he's so small," I said a few moments later as we stood in front of Vermeer's painting *The Milkmaid*. The entire painting, frame and all, couldn't have been more than two feet tall and a foot and a half wide. The painting's petiteness was even more amazing because of the detail Vermeer managed to include.

Noelle commented on how Vermeer chose for his subject a simple-looking young woman. She was carrying out the everyday task of pouring a stream of milk from a pitcher into a bowl on a cloth-covered table. A loaf of bread, complete with tiny seeds and fresh-baked cracks, sat in a detailed woven basket on the table. The milkmaid was dressed in common clothing for the sixteen hundreds, and yet the blues and yellows in her garments seemed textured and vivid, down to each fold.

"The milk looks real," I said. "As if it's actually being poured out of the pitcher. How did he do that?"

"Look at the broken pane in the window and the faint shadow on the nail in the wall. Such minute details. Amazing. It seems more like a photograph than a painting, doesn't it?"

"What are those designs at the bottom of the wall at the floor line?" I asked.

"Delft tiles. That's where he lived. The town of Delft was famous for its hand-painted ceramics, especially tiles. We should go there tomorrow. I think you would like it."

"Look at her. She appears to be concentrating hard on her task. So determined and yet so calm. She's at peace in the sacredness of the everyday." I looked over at Noelle's profile beside me. "She reminds me of you."

"It must be the buxom figure." Noelle stuck out her less-than-ample chest.

We hadn't realized another observer had entered the room and was standing only a few feet behind me. Noelle saw him when she turned toward me. I heard the man shuffle behind me and realized why Noelle's skin had taken on a sudden rosy tint.

"Moving on," Noelle urged under her breath.

We made the rounds of the room, marveling at each demure oil painting. Vermeer completed only about thirty-five paintings in his career. Each seemed crafted with extraordinary care for the smallest details. Light and shadows were his strengths.

"What are these paintings saying to you?" Noelle asked as we neared the end of the collection on display.

"What are they saying to me? I'm not sure. They're probably speaking Dutch." I grinned.

"No, I think they're speaking a universal language. Home and people and… What was it you said about the holiness of the everyday setting?"

I didn't remember saying anything about holiness, so I shrugged and nodded for her to go on with her interpretation.

"It's the light, isn't it? I was admiring the light coming through the window in each of the paintings."

We stood together, focusing on the light that poured through the unlatched window in the painting in front of us. The glass panes were thick and slightly distorted. An orderly set of lines ran through the pane, dividing the glass into individual boxes. Each pane seemed to have its own vibrancy and variation of light.

We made another slow walk around the room and noticed how often Vermeer used the same window, always on the left side, and how often the subject was presented facing the window. Even though the details in the windowpane and frame varied, the use of the light from that window was clearly a tool this artist liked.

I didn't know what that meant, but then I remembered Noelle's words about observing and admiring instead of trying to explain or evaluate.

Before leaving the museum, we stopped at the gift shop and bought postcards and note cards. I also purchased a book on Vermeer. As I stood in line to pay, I shuffled through the postcards of the paintings we had seen and said to Noelle, "So you really don't remember sending me this postcard ages ago?"

She shook her head. "I did remember the painting when we were standing there looking at it. And I do remember writing to you from Amsterdam, but I don't remember which postcard I sent you."

She reached for the postcard of *The Milkmaid* in my stack.

"What if I hadn't moved to Holland? What if you and I had found a way to go to New York instead?"

"We would have had very different lives."

Noelle nodded and handed the postcard back to me. "I like the way things turned out."

"So do I."

The sky had changed dramatically from when we first had entered the museum. Plenty of daylight remained, but the ever-busy clouds had been pulled taut and smoothed out into sheer sheets of white, as thin as a wedding veil. Strips of the wedding-veil clouds, cut with rounded edges and long trains, were scattered here and there over Amsterdam like remnants on the cutting-room floor of a master wedding gown designer. God was the Dutch master of the sky over Amsterdam.

My feet were tired, my head was pounding, and I was ready to wind down. Noelle talked me into taking a canal tour inside a long, low, covered boat. We bought some bottles of water, which helped with the headache.

As we peered out the windows, the guide described in three languages the different parts of the city we were cruising through.

The view in every direction was enchanting. Out the front of the tour barge, we watched the light from the late afternoon sun as it played on the water. In the same way that Vermeer had brought vibrancy to his paintings with unobtrusive dots of white at the corner of a mouth or an eye or in the sheen of a pearl ear-ring, God's touches of pure light on the water and through the green leaves of the trees brought life and peace.

Each footbridge we floated under was alive with bikes, pedestrians, and baby strollers. The houses on either side of the canal continued to amaze me with their steady posture, chin-up attitude, and ample windows.

"This is a little different from our earlier float down a canal," I said, "although I have a feeling I enjoyed our first trip quite a bit more than you did."

"I couldn't believe how relaxed you were in the midst of all the drama."

"I was just enjoying the ride. Even though I *float* through the *canal* of the shadow of death, I will fear no evil."

"You're getting pretty good at those paraphrases."

"Thanks. Or should I say 'bedankt'?"

"Listen to you! You're practically fluent in Dutch."

The tour guide came on the speaker and drew our attention to a bridge that led to a street as charming as all the others we had passed. He pointed out that was the direction of the red-light district.

"Someone always asks where it is," he said. "So there it is. And before you ask about the famous coffee shops of Amsterdam, I will emphasize that marijuana and other soft drugs are not legal in the Netherlands or in Amsterdam. But they are, as we like to call it, 'officially tolerated.' You may order them from a menu at these coffee shops, but you cannot order coffee there. For coffee you must go to a café or a restaurant. And if you want a handgun for your own private use, you won't find it in Amsterdam. You'll have to go to the U.S. for that."

I looked at Noelle, checking her expression to make sure what the guide had said wasn't an attempt at a bad joke.

She gave a small nod, as if she knew what my eyes were asking. Soft drugs and prostitution were "officially tolerated" in Amsterdam, but guns were not.

I thought of the different views of the world and of life that had confronted me since arriving in this unassuming country only a few days ago. The Netherlands was brimming with images, experiences, and ideas that never had touched me when I was home in my safe and protected corner of Ohio. I needed time to sort everything out and to decide how I felt about this wider view of how other people in the world lived.

We disembarked from the tour boat, and Noelle asked if I would like to see more of the city. "We could stop for something to eat at a café or keep exploring."

"It would be one of the cafés that serves real coffee," I added in view of the comments the guide had made on the canal boat.

"Yes, of course." She gave me an odd look, as if she wasn't making the same connection to the café that I had.

"Does it ever bother you that the government looks the other way on drugs and the red-light district?"

She nodded, not so much in agreement, it seemed, but more in recognition of where my train of thought was headed. "One thing I learned early on living here is that Dutch people have a strong tolerance for differences. Freedom is highly valued here."

"Individual freedom, right?"

"Yes, you could say that. The mind-set of this pragmatic culture is along the lines of 'live and let live.' When individual freedoms are honored, peace prevails."

I wasn't sure how I felt about some of the things Noelle said, but I didn't have the brain space to sort out my opinions at the moment. I didn't know enough about how politics were set up in a country such as the Netherlands, where the country's figurehead was a queen and the decisions were made by parliament. Politics weren't my idea of a great topic to pursue, so I circled back to her earlier suggestion that we find a café.

"Food sounds like a very good idea."

What happened next is the sort of thing that occurs in any country when a gathering of family or friends includes everyone who is too tired or too hungry—or both—to think clearly. Neither of us could pull off a suggestion that sounded appealing, so we opted to take the train and head to Noelle's.

By the time we had wound our way back to the beautiful, brick central train station, it was commute time once again, and the area swarmed with business travelers. Even so, both of us were content with our decision to call it a day rather than meander around Amsterdam without a clear objective.

The only disagreeable part was that we were both very hungry. While Noelle figured out our return train tickets, I stood eying the possibilities inside an extensive vending machine. It was a cafeteria-style rotating food selector rather than the candy bar vending machines I was familiar with. Rotating cubicles with plastic dividers held sandwiches and other food selections for purchase.

"What are those?" I asked Noelle, pointing at what looked like fat, breaded fish sticks.

"*Kroketten.* You don't want one."

"I don't?"

She made a face and shook her head. "They are typically Dutch, but, no, you don't want one. They are sort of like eating a deep-fried sausage made of who-knows-what—horse hoofs? Not recommended. Let's get some *stroopwafels* instead. Come. They have a good place for them down at the other end of the station. They're fresh and hot."

The lunch wagon–style grill just outside the station looked questionable to me. I couldn't imagine that the food that came from the trailer would be better than the food offered inside the station in the industrial-looking dispenser.

Noelle ordered for us, and I didn't even ask her what a stroopwafel was.

It turned out to be a cookie, or at least what I would call a cookie. They were warm, as promised, and delicious. Just like the hint in the name, the stroopwafel looked like two mini, flat waffles pressed together. In between the wafer-thin layers was a sweet, drippy syrup. I still could smell the brown sugary scent of the treat after we were on the train.

Jelle had dinner ready for us when we shuffled into the house. He had made pasta and salad and in his self-effacing way pointed out it wasn't on caliber with his fish from my first night. Noelle lit the candles, and we gathered at the table.

Reserved Jelle had no idea what to do with us once we got a bit of dinner in us and felt our spirits revive. He made the mistake of asking, "What did you do while you were in Amsterdam?"

We recounted for him silly detail by silly detail of how the two of us led the Sisterchicks in Wooden Shoes parade down the canal.

"She waved at people," Noelle playfully tattled on me.

Jelle looked from his wife to me without changing his expression. It seemed he was trying to decide what to believe.

"It's true. While your wife risked her life to grab the rescue rope and save us, I waved to the people. It was the most fun I've had in a long time."

"There's more," Noelle said. "Tourists were taking her photo."

"Our photos." I motioned to the two of us. "We were in this together, you know."

"Oh, trust me, I know."

"What do you think these people are going to do with your photos?" Jelle asked.

Noelle and I looked at each other, and I said, "Show their friends, I imagine. I told Noelle this would be our fifteen seconds of fame."

Jelle pushed back from the table, his pasta finished. "Before we have coffee, I must check on something." He was on his way up the stairs when he called down, "I stopped at the bakery and bought stoopwafels for dessert. I thought Summer would like to try them."

Noelle and I exchanged glances. Neither of us volunteered that we had stopped for warm ones a few hours earlier.

While Noelle started the coffee in the modern-looking espresso machine, I cleared the table. She set up the serving tray with the cream, sugar, and coffee cups and handed it to me. "Let's have coffee in the living room. I'll bring the 'very special' dessert."

We exchanged grins. I had just placed the serving tray on the coffee table when Jelle came down the spiral stairs with an open laptop in his hands. "Noelle, come. Have a look."

She leaned in to see the screen with her eyes squinted. As I watched her face, her eyes grew wide.

"Oh, Summer Breeze, wait until you see this! Our fifteen seconds of fame has gone global!"

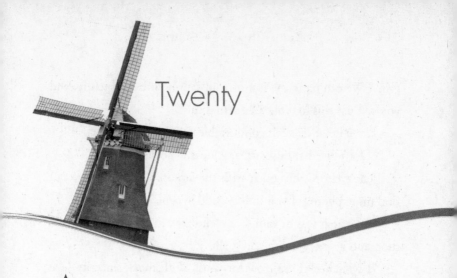

Twenty

Apparently it took Jelle very little effort to find us on a young American woman's blog about her vacation in Amsterdam. I don't know what key phrase he entered under "images on the Web" to bring us up, but there we were. A couple of Sisterchicks in a wooden shoe. Noelle had her back to the camera, but I was facing the photographer.

And I was waving.

I had no idea I looked so ridiculous. Well, I suppose I had some inkling. But seeing the photo in that cartoonish wooden-shoe boat, with my goofy grin and my hair going every which way...well, it was hilarious. I couldn't deny the shot was laughable.

"I can't believe how many ridiculous pictures have been taken of me since I arrived! First with the sea gulls and now this."

"You are making your visit memorable," Jelle said with a little-boy grin on his face. "Memorable for many people."

"If my children had any idea what I was doing this week...or Wayne! Wayne will never let me out of the house again!"

"I will e-mail you the link." Jelle's face still sported a cheery grin. "We can paste the rest of your family into the picture, and you can use this for your Christmas card."

I loved that Jelle felt comfortable enough to tease me.

"Don't give her husband any ideas," Noelle said.

Jelle went to the couch with the laptop. "Let's see if we can find more photos of you in the wooden shoe."

His search was in vain, but it didn't matter. We had the one shot, and it pretty much said it all.

"I will check tomorrow for you." With mock sincerity Jelle added, "My fees are good."

"Your fees?" I asked.

He turned to Noelle and stated something in Dutch. She replied in Dutch, and he turned to me, ready to make his meaning clear.

"I have a discount this week on my fees for blackmail."

I laughed. Jelle seemed pleased with himself.

We calmed the conversation down and sipped the coffee. Jelle held out the plate of stroopwafels. I took one, thanked him, and bit demurely into it.

Remembering the hand motion Noelle had shown me when I first had arrived and we ate the delicious apple tart, I put my open palm to the side of my ear and slowly waved my hand back and forth, as if I were fluffing up my hair.

"Leper," I said.

Jelle went from looking almost impressed to looking surprised.

Noelle burst out laughing.

"Uh-oh. What did I say?"

"You said 'leper,' " Noelle told me. "Like a person with leprosy. I don't think that's how you wanted to describe Jelle's special treat."

"No. Definitely not. What was the word you used the other day when you looked like you were fluffing up your hair?"

"*Lekker.* It means 'delicious.' "

"Yes. That's what I was going for. Delicious. Lekker."

Jelle looked thoroughly entertained. I was content to know that I had provided the dear guy with so much to laugh about. I was sure he would remember me long after my visit.

As I headed up the stairs to my guest room for the night, Jelle called out, *"Slaap lekker."*

I turned to Noelle for translation. I was pretty sure he had said "lekker," but what was he calling delicious?

"He's telling you to sleep deliciously."

I laughed as if it were one of his clever sarcasms.

"He's not making a joke," Noelle assured me. "We say that here. Slaap lekker. Sleep deliciously."

"Well then, slaap lekker to both of you as well."

"Very good!" Noelle pointed at me. "You just proved you are no longer a Dutch language school dropout. Well done."

"Thank you. And by the way, at what time do I show up for classes tomorrow morning?"

"Breakfast will be fruit and bread, and it will be available for you anytime after seven."

The next morning Jelle announced over the dark coffee he had made to accompany our fruit and bread that he had decided to accompany us to Delft. "For protection."

"Are you saying you need to protect your wife from me?" I asked.

"I am saying I need to protect both of you from owners of floating wooden shoes that you just happen to meet along the canals."

"We learned our lesson," I said. "We'll avoid mishaps this time. I promise."

Noelle gave me a wary look. "Based on our record, I'm not sure we can make such a promise."

"You're right. I have been a little more event prone than I ever am at home."

Jelle rubbed his hands together as if I had just announced I was treating him to a big, fat, juicy steak for dinner. "If that is the situation, then I think I will come along just for the photo opportunity."

At the end of all his teasing, Jelle went to work, and Noelle and I took our chances visiting another city without his protection. We did have to promise that we would provide full disclosure of any and all photos of any and all mishaps along the way.

He said he was going to start his own blog and my visit would be his premier topic.

"I honestly think I got all my mishaps over with during the last few days," I said. "Today will be boring. Nothing blogworthy will happen."

Jelle kissed Noelle good-bye. "If the two of you have more expensive damages today, I want to know about it."

"I told you I don't plan to provide any more blog material," I said.

"No. I want to know for my credit card company. I have to

make sure I have a big enough line of credit for the charges if you're going to lose any more bicycles in the canals."

Noelle playfully pushed him out the door, and we organized ourselves for the drive to Delft. I felt bad about the expenses that had added up since I had arrived and offered to pay her for gas. Noelle assured me Delft wasn't far, so I should drop my insistence about paying for the petrol. She also said she had a secret parking area she knew about that charged less than the high-rise parking.

As fun as the train had been on previous days, I was glad we were in sweet little Bluebell once again and puttering down the roads that were becoming familiar. I'm sure my deep American roots prompted my response, but having your own car on call whenever you need it gives you a sense of independence. I knew it was possible that my grasp at all things independent could fall under the category of needing to be more in control. Whatever the reason, I was relieved when Noelle said we would drive today.

The other reason I was grateful we were driving was because I had rubbed a blister the day before with all the walking we had done. I had taken care of it that morning and made sure I had extra bandages with me, but my heel still was sore. I was hoping the amateur first-aid job would help me not to rub the same spot.

Outside, the day was shaping up to be pleasant with clear skies. In the few days since I had arrived, it seemed clear that spring was coming to stay. Flowers seemed to be popping up everywhere—along the road, in planter boxes under windows, and even in front of highway signs.

I couldn't prove my theory, but the grape hyacinth seemed to be a deeper shade of blue here than at home. The daffodils definitely hung on longer than where I lived. In various shaded areas, where an entire bulb garden burst out of a barrel planter or a painted box, I noticed a number of deep yellow daffys still blowing their trumpets beside the unfolding tulips.

The tour book was right. Spring was the time to visit the Netherlands. The best time, I'm sure. Although I would be curious to return in the heat of the summer and see what the beaches on the North Sea are like with swarms of visitors. The long stretch of eating places that edged the pale sand indicated that the place would be hopping with business when the weather was conducive.

As we drove closer to Delft, Noelle pointed out another windmill in the distance. The landscape was so flat it was easy to make out the distinct shape of the four arms. This particular windmill looked like the front of a single-engine airplane that had made a perfect landing on top of a grain silo and had decided to stay there. The variety of windmill styles surprised me.

"You live in a beautiful place, Noelle."

"Yes, I think so too. I don't like a few things, but any place has its list of drawbacks as well as positives."

"What don't you like about living here?"

"Some winters are worse than others. I grew up with snow in Wyoming, so I don't mind the cold and wind so much. What I have a hard time with are those bleak, freezing days when the sky is gray, gray, gray. One or two such days here and there I don't mind. I make soup and bread and wear my wool socks around the house all day. But some winters we have weeks of gray. That's when I miss the wild, blue, winter skies of Wyoming."

Noelle had been inching her way down a narrow street in part of what I assumed was Delft. It was a close stretch of bumpy road, but she managed to fit Bluebell into an end parking space.

"So this is your secret parking lot?" I looked at the backs of rundown buildings that appeared to have been built right after the war but never had received any more attention.

"Not much to look at, but it works."

We locked up the car and were on our way to see the city of Delft. Within a few blocks I could tell I was rubbing the bandage off my heel.

"Could we go back to the car? I need to fix this bandage."

We turned around and retraced our steps to the parking area. While I took off my shoe and peeled off my sock, Noelle made a phone call. She was watching my paramedic skills and at one point made a face. Reaching around me and opening the glove compartment, she took out a small first-aid kit and handed it to me. With the phone pulled away from her ear for a moment, she said, "You'll find some first-aid cream and plasters in there."

I wasn't sure what a plaster was but quickly figured it out. Her plasters, or Band-Aids, were larger than mine and covered the area with a much firmer sticking power.

"All set." I put the kit back in the glove compartment.

She was still on her cell but mostly listening. With a nod Noelle locked up the car, and we started on our way into the center of Delft once again.

As we strolled down a canal road similar to the ones we had traversed yesterday, Noelle continued her call. I didn't mind that she was multitasking, leading the tour into Delft while being on her phone. She had hardly been on the phone any of the other days we had been sightseeing. I knew that if she were visiting me, the opposite would be the case. I was on my phone a lot with our children when I was home.

I wondered if any of my children had called while I was gone. I was sure the girls had checked in with Wayne. All three of them had a soft spot for their dad. I wondered what Wayne had told them. I had left in such a flurry all I did was send a short e-mail to them, saying that an opportunity had come up for me to go to the Netherlands to meet Noelle. I gave the days and times of my flights and told them I loved them. That was all. Short and sweet, as if what I was doing weren't out of the ordinary.

As we walked over a footbridge spanning a canal, I stopped and took in the view. Noelle stopped walking and stood a few feet away, finishing her phone call.

The houses that lined the canal road were similar to the ones we had seen in Amsterdam. But these houses seemed more ornately decorated. The colors were deeper, more jewel toned than the brighter trims on the brick houses in Amsterdam.

A movie I had seen a long time ago came to mind. I couldn't remember the name of it, but it was a spy movie with a ring of international thieves. The objective was to break into a safe in a house along a canal in Amsterdam.

As I looked at the row of Delft homes from the footbridge, it seemed as if the movie could have been filmed right on this spot. This neighborhood had the same feel as the charming stretch of canal and restored homes in the spy movie.

Also I realized I was becoming so acclimated to the architecture and layout of the canals that everything was beginning to feel familiar. Whatever the reason, I loved the view.

A playful breeze waltzed by, ruffling up the trees and tossing a handful of their pink confetti into the air. In the canal below us, two white swans floated and preened in the blossom-strewn waters.

I was standing in the middle of a fairy tale.

Noelle was apologetic once she was off the phone. "I wouldn't have stayed on so long, but I wasn't able to get off right away."

"That's okay. It didn't bother me a bit. Look at the swans. Look at this view. I should take a picture."

"I'm sorry. It's a rude thing to do around company."

"Honestly, Noelle, I wasn't offended. Here. Stand right there, and let me take a picture of you."

She smiled, but my viewfinder seemed to pick up an unsettled look in her eyes.

"You okay?" I snapped another shot of the swans floating in the pink confetti–laced waters.

"Yes. I was getting the update on Zahida."

"How is she?"

"Quite good, actually. Her decision is set. She's not going to return to her home or her family. They made it clear that she's being cut off from them." Noelle's expression tightened. "That's a very difficult thing for a woman under any circumstance. She's so young."

When Noelle made the comment, I saw a halo of sadness in her eyes. The connection between her leaving home at eighteen and never returning closely coincided with Zahida's situation. I could hear the empathy in Noelle's voice. More important, I could see it in her eyes.

"Come." Now I was the one who had picked up Noelle's quick, to-the-point phrase. "Even though I walk over a footbridge into the town of Delft, I will fear no evil…"

Noelle spontaneously looped her arm around my neck and gave me an unexpected kiss on the side of my head. "You are the best medicine. You know that, don't you? The Bible says that laughter is the best medicine but—"

"Actually, the verse in Proverbs says that a merry heart does good like medicine. I looked it up once."

"Fine. Now hush. I'm giving you a compliment."

I laughed at her brash reprimand.

"Okay, so the Bible says that a merry heart does us good like medicine. The point is, you have been like medicine for me. Your visit, the timing, and everything have been just right. I needed this. You're a gift to me, Summer. You really are."

My eyes teared up. "You're a gift to me too, Noelle. You always have been."

We hugged each other and strolled into the old city like old friends, joined at the heart.

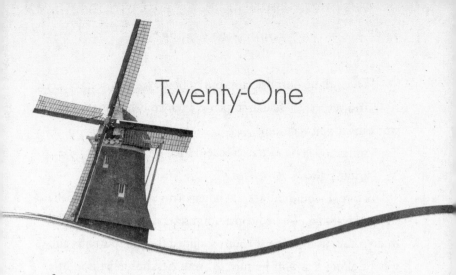

Twenty-One

I want to take you to the market square first," Noelle said. "After being in Saint Bavo's Cathedral in Haarlem, you should see the church here."

I wasn't sure I wanted to visit another church. Not that I minded where we went particularly. "All I ask is that we see some Delft tiles before the day is done."

"We will."

"That's the only thing I remember you telling me about Delft. They make tiles here."

"Yes, they do, and they have for hundreds of years. Remember we saw them in Vermeer's paintings? We can go to a place where on some days you can watch the craftsmen paint the tiles."

"Wonderful."

"I also want to take you to a *pannenkoekenhuis*."

"Okay," I said slowly. "Do I want to know what a pan-a-kook-whatever is?"

Noelle's lighthearted air was returning. "I think I'll keep you wondering."

"That's right. Surprises are your hobby."

"And you are allergic to suspense. I remember. Don't worry. I won't make you wait long."

"You're too good to me, Noelle-o Mell-o."

"Quite right."

Before I could muster a noteworthy comeback, Noelle stopped walking. We had come upon several shops and decided to do some meandering. I hadn't shopped for any souvenirs and was thinking it would be nice if I returned home with a little something for Wayne and each of the kids. But what?

The first shop was filled with Delft pottery. The distinct, hand-painted blue tiles and pottery were intriguing because each piece was slightly different. The scenes painted by hand on the white tiles included windmills, canals, cows, milkmaids, boys ice-skating on canals, and, of course, wooden shoes.

I had selected four tiles and then put them back. They were heavy. Since we had to pass this shop when we returned to the car, it seemed wise to do my buying at the end of the day rather than haul everything around with me for hours.

The next shop we explored sold kitchen gadgets and a gourmet assortment of what Noelle called "stinky cheese."

"We can sample anything. If you see one you would like to try, tell me."

It seemed pretty early in the day for sampling cheese, especially when it was presented as stinky. What I did love about the shop was the understated beauty of how everything was lined up on the shelves and how the rounds of cheese were displayed in the refrigerated case in the center of the store. Everything was just so.

I felt as if I had walked into a modern still life by one of the Dutch masters. Once again it was the common, everyday setting and the people that formed the composition. But the orderliness of the "props" and the soft light through the windows elevated even this cheese shop to a level where I felt touched by a hazy sense of the eternal.

I stood with my head tilted, gazing at the way the light came in through the high windows and changed the visual effect of a shiny metal nutcracker. The gadget was on display next to a very large round of Gouda cheese, so marked with the name on the red wax casing. Next to the nutcracker was a small bowl of walnuts available for demonstrating the nutcracker's handiness and for sampling the nuts, along with carefully cut squares of cheese. A clean, empty white dish stood ready to the side, a willing receptacle for the unwanted walnut shells.

Noelle sidled up to me and followed my line of sight. "What are you looking at?"

"The sacredness of the everyday," was the answer that tumbled out. I didn't expect to say that. I didn't know I had even thought that line. But there it was. I was an appreciative observer of the sacredness of the everyday.

Turning to Noelle I asked, "Was that line used at one of the museums yesterday in connection with one of the Dutch painters?"

"No, I think you used that term when we were watching the milkmaid pour from her pitcher."

"That's right. Her simple act seemed so pristinely noble."

"You said she was reflecting the sacredness of the everyday or something like that."

She nodded toward the dish of small Gouda samples. "Did you try the cheese? Gouda is made in the Netherlands. In the south. It has more of a mild taste than sharp. Some varieties taste a little smoky to me. You should try some. It's going to be more distinct than what you would find at home."

I still was basking in the thought about the sacredness of the everyday. Every day unfolded with moments when the eternal seemed to touch the temporal. Light overcame darkness. Hope triumphed over despair. Nothing here in the earthly realm changed. But God somehow touched people, places, and moments, and the everyday became a glimpse of heaven.

"It's like Corrie and the Hiding Place," I said to Noelle, ignoring her offer of cheese. "Or the tulip fields. Or even the painting of our little milkmaid. Common, yes. Unsuspecting, yes. But so beautiful. Like a glimpse of heaven out of the corner of your eye."

Noelle leaned back and examined my expression.

"The sacredness of the everyday," I repeated since she obviously wasn't on the same track I was on. I had left her standing on the platform and was riding this train of thought as far as it would take me.

She didn't say anything. That was one of Noelle's traits I was coming to appreciate. She was good at just being. She didn't require a lot of details or explanations. Nor did she offer many of the same. But her actions and her words matched up.

Noelle was a living example of the sacredness of the everyday.

With a slow-rising grin she said, "You are learning to be Dutch, Summer. You say what you think, put it out there for discussion. That's how we do it."

I didn't know if I was ready to put a lot of my thoughts out there for discussion, but this one clear thought comforted me. The sacredness of the everyday. God allowed us little glimpses of heaven here on earth.

"Noelle, do you have any paper? I need to remember this."

"I think so." She rifled through her purse and pulled out a small flip notepad. Adding a pen in the other hand, she said, "Go ahead. I'll take notes. What do you want to remember?"

I reiterated the thoughts about the sacredness of the everyday and how these glimpses of beauty are moments when the eternal breaks through into the temporal.

"Got it," Noelle said, reading the notes she had taken.

"Here's my other thought. Write this down too, will you? Is it possible that planted inside each of us is a yearning for heaven? Is that why we're drawn to beauty and sacredness whenever we find it in temporal things?"

Noelle tore off the pages from her notebook. "Your thoughts, my friend."

I looked at what she had written and felt warmed. With so much of our communication being via e-mail, it had been a long time since I'd seen Noelle's familiar, slanted cursive writing. In all our years of exchanging thoughts, we'd never had this luxury of completing the thought and writing it for a personal hand-off.

I would treasure this simple piece of paper. Not so much because of my formulating thoughts that were recorded there, but because Noelle had written them and then handed the paper to me.

"Now, to complete your moment of personal enlightenment, I still think you should try some of this cheese."

"Okay, which one should I try first?"

Noelle stuck with her original suggestion of trying the Gouda.

I chewed the small square slowly and thought of the young, grateful woman who had sat across from me at the farm. The taste of the soft, mild cheese was similar to the simple jack cheese I bought at home by the pound. Although the Gouda had a deeper flavor. A broader aftertaste.

"Do you like it?"

I nodded. What I liked more than the taste of the cheese was that all my senses were involved. This seemed to be a high value for Noelle and Jelle, as I had learned from my meals with them. Food was not for wolfing down so you could run out the door refueled. Meals were for conversation and fellowship. Food was for enjoyment and discovery of tastes and textures and lingering sensations on the palette.

The Gouda certainly left a lingering sensation on my palette. We moved on to a more-intense-flavored white cheese followed by a cracker. In five minutes Noelle had led me on a circular tour of Dutch cheese, and we were back where we had started, by the refrigerated case with the Gouda.

In the same way she didn't ask me at the museum which painting I liked best, she didn't ask for an evaluation of the cheeses. The experience seemed to be simply for the opportunity to observe, taste, and appreciate.

I wanted to cap off the moment somehow. I had just experienced a sampling of God's immense creation. My mind was in a place of appreciating the Lord's everyday goodness, even in such things as stinky cheese and light coming through a store window. I felt the need for the equivalent of an amen to this everyday act of worship.

What sufficed for the moment was the use of the nutcracker and a single, perfectly balanced walnut. It cracked right down the middle. The nutmeat fell into my hand, and with that, my sense of taste seemed to say, "Amen."

Noelle collected a few things in the shop to buy. I didn't. Again, I didn't want to carry heavy items around with me all day. She seemed used to doing this sort of shopping and walking, which once again explained why she was decidedly fitter than I.

Then I glanced at the nutcracker. The sun had moved, or perhaps it was I who had moved the nutcracker out of the direct path of the light. The metal no longer lit up with that hint of the sacred that had captured my thoughts when we first entered the shop.

I wanted to remember that. It wasn't the nutcracker that was holy. It was the touch of the eternal that bathed the utensil with light. It was the momentary reflection of that light that made the common tool beautiful.

In a way that I still can't explain, I felt as if I understood what it was like to be an ordinary nutcracker. I was nothing out of the ordinary. But whenever the eternal touches me, I know that I warm and maybe even glow a little. I am one of God's everyday women. But He makes me sacred.

We were about to leave the store when I stopped and thought for a moment. "Just a minute," I told Noelle and went back to buy the nutcracker.

We left the lovely stinky cheese shop and strode across the wide-open market square.

"You liked that little nutcracker, didn't you?" Noelle's voice was sweet and motherly.

"Yes, I did. It reminded me of one my mom had. She used to bring it out every autumn along with a special wooden bowl that she filled with nuts. It was a big deal whenever we got to use the nutcracker to crack our own walnuts and almonds." I knew the memory was simple, but it made me feel close to my mom, and that was what made it golden.

"You had a wonderful mom," Noelle said.

"Yes, I did."

"I remember something you wrote about her years ago after one of your miscarriages, something about waiting with empty hands."

I nodded. "I remember writing to you about that day. It was a huge moment for me. I think I was only twenty-four. I thought God had abandoned me."

As we walked across the open square, I reminisced about how my mom had come over to our apartment with a batch of fresh-baked cookies. She had looked into my eyes and said, "Summer, I know you are carrying this loss as if it is yours alone to bear. But you were not meant to carry such a heavy burden. Give it back to God and keep giving it back until you have no more grief in your heart to hand over to Him. Then wait and see what gift He places in your empty hands."

Noelle summarized the memory for me by saying, "And now,

all these years later, we know what God placed in your empty hands. Six children."

I shook my head. "No, not six children."

Noelle stopped walking and looked at me. "Did I count wrong, or did you only rent those scrub-faced children every year to pose with you and Wayne for your Christmas cards?"

I smiled. "No, they're all mine. I claim each and every one of them. But the true answer is that after the first two miscarriages, God placed in my empty hands a third miscarriage."

Noelle's expression turned somber. "I forgot about the third one."

"That one was the hardest, I think. By that time no one really entered into the grieving with me. One friend told Wayne and me it was time for us to take a hint or get a clue or something along those lines. He and his wife had two children, and they hadn't experienced a miscarriage, so he didn't know what he was saying. But my point is, after double sadness God gave me more sadness. After that, He gave me joy."

"Joy times six," Noelle reminded me.

"Yes. Double what I had lost."

Twenty-Two

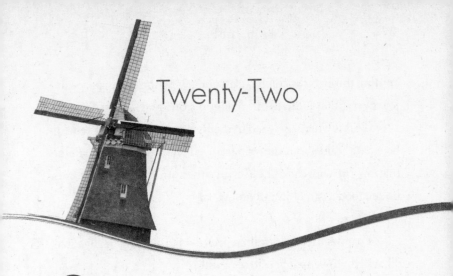

Our conversation concluded just as we arrived at the front of the New Church at the far end of the town square.

"I wanted you to see inside," Noelle said.

After the feast for my eyes and an awakening of my thoughts toward all things majestic that I had experienced at Saint Bavo, I couldn't wait to see the inside of the large church in Delft.

An entrance fee was requested. Noelle paid for both of us in the sectioned-off entrance, where a modest selection of books was offered in several languages.

We walked through a wooden door and entered the huge, open sanctuary. I was prepared to be awed.

Instead, I was stunned. Shocked. The cavernous church was void of any art, color, or decorations.

My jaw had dropped. "What happened?"

"What happened to what?"

"This church. It's vacant. Where's all the amazing art? Those used to be stained-glass windows, right? The sun should be coming through the colored glass and giving this huge space some joy. Everything in here is the color of stone gray."

"This is what happened in the Reformation. Do you remember what I said about the iconoclasts? The riots during the Reformation rid churches like this of anything that could be misunderstood as an object of idol worship."

"Wow."

"I know. It's a stark difference to what we saw in Haarlem. That's why I wanted you to see this."

I felt angry. "Who were these iconoclasts? Were we looking at their faces yesterday at the Rijksmuseum?"

Noelle said that she wasn't up on her Dutch history, that we could buy a book on our way out, and it would help explain that era. "Although, each author will add his opinion of history, so it depends on which author you read and how he spins the details."

"Why would anyone strip away all that is uplifting and beautiful?"

"I'm not sure we can understand how out of control religion was during that era. The poor were trying to buy their way to heaven. The crafters of all that was ornate were trying to outdo each other in creating religious imagery. I'm sure it was complicated."

At times like this I realized how limited my knowledge and view of the world and of history were.

"You know," Noelle added, "to put in a good word for the reformists, they could be viewed as well-meaning purists. They were trying to direct worshipers away from the material trappings and help them focus only on God, who is invisible and cannot and should not be represented in man's likeness."

"True, but what about everything I was just saying in the cheese shop? Art and beauty are what give us those glimpses of the eternal."

"And what happens when the art becomes the object of the worship instead of the One the art is supposed to represent?"

"Then the art was overdone, or at least the meaning attached to the art was allowed to be overemphasized. Obviously, it got out of control."

Noelle quickly countered. "So the art was too good? Is that what you're saying? The beauty was too convincing?"

"No, the art and beauty were what became tangible. Visible. We hold on to what we know and what we can see. Not what is out there in the eternal realm."

"And that should be an acceptable excuse for the corruption?"

"No, of course not. The focus of the worshipers got off center. Obviously."

"And what a good thing that never happens today." It was easy to detect the subtle bite of sarcasm in Noelle's voice.

I didn't have a retort for her. I had listened to Noelle and Jelle talk like this a few nights ago with a volley of questions and no sense that a final answer was needed. With Wayne, closure on a topic was important. Rarely did he and I leave an issue "out there on the table," as Noelle called it, to keep pushing it back and forth. Wayne and I liked conclusions.

In a small way I was beginning to understand the cultural

mind-set that had startled me on the canal tour yesterday. "Officially tolerated" was the term the canal guide had used for the government's position on the questionably moral activities available in Amsterdam.

The moral and religious pendulum had swung so far to the right and left in generations past. Did this generation, still recovering from the horrors of World War II, prefer any option that favored peace?

I took a seat in one of the plain wooden pews and looked around. Noelle sat beside me.

"It's complicated, isn't it?" I stated.

"More than you or I know. If you really want to bend your mind with some history, think about where the Puritans came from before they landed on Plymouth Rock."

"Do you mean the pilgrims?"

"Yes. The pilgrims who landed at Plymouth Rock and became the forerunners of the rights of religious freedom in the U.S. Do you know where they came from?"

"England."

"Originally, yes. But many of them fled England due to religious restrictions. They came here. Literally. To Delft. That first group of pilgrims sought religious freedom here in Delft for twenty years or so. When they weren't able to worship the way they wanted, they sailed from Delft back to England, and in England they boarded the *Mayflower* and sailed to America."

"I never knew that."

"If you can believe this, I did a report on the pilgrims when I was in high school, and that's where I learned some of this. It was long before I ever imagined I would come to the Netherlands."

"Why did you write the report? I mean, what prompted your interest?"

"My dad's side of the family can trace back to an ancestor who came over on the *Mayflower*."

"Really? So you may have an ancestor who actually came to this church while living in Delft."

Noelle's eyes widened. "I never thought of that."

"You could be related to someone who sat right here in this pew hundreds of years ago."

Now her facial expression definitely was sober.

With a sweeping gesture at our surroundings, I said, "What have we learned in all these centuries? I mean, where is the balance in all this?" My voice echoed in the cavernous sanctuary.

Noelle didn't respond.

"There has to be some way to balance the opulent misuse of money, power, and materialism in Christianity and yet not go all the way to this stark, depressing vacantness."

"Well, when you find that balance, be sure to enlighten the rest of the world. It's a problem that never has gone away."

"I know. I just never saw it as clearly as I have since I've been here. They threw the daddy out with the bathwater."

"Did you say 'daddy'?"

"No, I said 'baby.' At least that's what I thought I said. Isn't that what I said? That's what I meant. They threw the baby out with the bathwater."

Noelle looked up at the solemn, gray, arched ceiling. She drew in a deep breath.

"You okay?"

She nodded. "Give me a minute, okay?"

I got up from the pew and left Noelle to her thoughts. I assumed she was pondering her puritanical roots. Or perhaps she still was mentally tossing back and forth the thoughts on materialism and art.

Content to wander a bit by myself, I wound my way back to the English-language books for sale in the narthex. Against my earlier mandate not to fill my shoulder bag with souvenirs, I bought a book on the Reformation.

I didn't have to wait long for Noelle. She joined me, and we stepped outside into a sprinkling of airy raindrops. We moved to the side of the church and stood under a narrow overhang where we buttoned up our coats.

Noelle looked up at the thin clouds sailing high above us. "This will pass." Without looking at me she said in a firm voice, "I finally did it, Summer."

"Did what?"

"I…"

I placed my hand on her arm and moved around so my open expression was readily in view.

Noelle lowered her gaze from the sky and looked at me with tears in her eyes. "I asked God to enable me to forgive my dad."

I looked at her with a steady gaze, encouraging her to keep talking.

"I've been thinking about this ever since the tour guide's talk at the Ten Boom house. I have no relationship with my father because I have not forgiven him. I've never felt I was able to forgive him. Not on my own power. Not by my own emotions."

She drew in a wobbly breath and flicked a runaway tear from her cheek. "And then you went and said what you did, and I felt like a javelin pierced my heart."

"What did I say?" I tried to recall how our back-and-forth conversation had gone inside the church. Had I offended her? Wasn't the ebb-and-flow style of opinion sharing exactly what Noelle said the Dutch favored?

"You said they threw the daddy out with the bathwater."

"I still think I said 'baby.'"

"No, you said 'daddy,' and that's what went through me, because that's exactly what I did. I started my own rebellion at eighteen, and I threw my daddy out of my life. That whole part of my life has been as stark, gray, and vacant as the inside of the church where we were just sitting. In my own puritanical sort of zeal, I threw out everything."

I gave her arm a comforting squeeze. I still had no idea what had caused the rift between Noelle and her father. Perhaps I never would know. That was fine. I didn't need to have the specifics on the cause of her longstanding pain.

But I did love being here, at this moment, under the eaves of this ancient church, protected from the rain and acutely connected to what was happening in Noelle's heart. She was opening her hands to the Lord and offering back to Him all her pain, just as my mother had admonished me to do so many years ago.

"And?" I softly nudged her to go on. I wanted to hear her say that God had met her in that moment as she sat in the pew. I wanted to know that in a moment of everyday sacredness she had extended forgiveness to her father and all was well in her heart.

"And what?" Noelle asked.

"What happened after you asked God to enable you to forgive your father?"

Noelle looked at me as if I had missed the point of her comments. "That was it. I asked Him to enable me. That was my prayer."

"And did He?"

"I don't know."

Her answer surprised me. I was accustomed to conclusions and happy endings, especially whenever God was involved in the story. Who doesn't love a testimony with a victorious ending?

Noelle, however, was perhaps more authentic and closer to the truth of the situation because of her willingness to wait on God. Her patience could be weighed on a different scale than the scale of immediacy that dominated my life.

"So, we wait and see," she said. "This would be a good time for your surprise."

I tried to switch gears. "The pan-a-kook surprise?"

"Yes." Noelle held her hand out and checked the raindrops. "It's all right. Follow me."

She took off across the square with her quick, long legs. I found it less difficult to keep up with her than on previous hikes. Amazing. In a few short days, Noelle had turned me into a walkin' woman. I couldn't help but wonder how different my life would be if I kept up this sort of walking once I returned home.

Then I remembered what else might give me a different life once I returned home. How could I learn to adopt Noelle's calm sense of patience of waiting on God without needing an immediate answer?

The rain stopped just as Noelle led me to the front of a restaurant that faced the large market square in the center of Delft.

"The pannenkoekenhuis."

I stared at the photos of the featured plates on the menu. "Pancakes?"

"Yes, pancakes. Pannenkoeken. I've been saving this experience for you. It's a very Dutch thing to have pancakes for lunch or dinner. Try saying it. Pannenkoeken. I thought it was one of the most fun words to pronounce when I first got here. As a matter of fact, my first job in Rotterdam was working at a pannenkoekenhuis."

"This was my big surprise?"

"Oh, I'm wounded! This is very Dutch. This is what we do. When we can't explain something or can't settle an argument, we go eat pancakes. It helps."

"Okay."

"You'll like them. Come."

Once we were seated at an outside table under the canvas canopy, Noelle added, "These aren't exactly like pancakes you eat at home. They're fancy."

Our table was in a great location because we were both facing the square, and it didn't feel as if anyone seated around us could hear our conversation. At so many of the other places we had eaten, it seemed we were sharing the meal with all the diners nearby. In a country with sixteen million people, I could see why privacy was rare and how learning to live and let live was useful.

The rain had cleared, and the returning sun caused the many spit-and-polish spots on the town square to glisten. The New Church was within our view at the far end of the square, and the town hall was at the opposite end of the square. Directly in front of us, at the other side of the large open area, was the line of shops we had first explored, including the stinky-cheese shop.

"These pancakes," Noelle went on to explain, "are more like crepes in thickness, although some of the varieties are nice and dense." She pointed at a picture on one of the laminated menus the waitress had handed us when we were seated. "They come with almost any kind of topping you can think of. Fruit, meat, cheese, sugar. Whatever you like."

It helped a lot that the menu included pictures of these celebrated pancakes. The picture of the one with cheese and mushroom topping looked more like a personal-sized pizza than a pancake.

I selected the one with apples and bacon.

"Do you want to order for me, Noelle? I'd like to see if they have a rest room I can use."

"Sure. If I remember correctly, the rest room is upstairs."

I entered the darkened restaurant and walked past the bar as if I knew where I was going. The stairs were easy enough to find. Once again the steps were steep and narrow. I bumped my head on the ascent and wondered how old this building was. It had to be several hundred years old if it had survived in its original condition and position on the edge of the market square.

The upstairs made it clear that renovations had been done to the property. I guessed this formerly had been a house, and since a modern, flushing toilet system had been installed on the second floor, it obviously had been adjusted to meet restaurant codes.

In keeping with the décor of the rest of the house, the bathroom was painted a warm yellow, and the edges of the mirror frame and doorframe had been painted black. I figured out all the slightly different systems in the bathroom—the flush system and the water faucet in the sink.

Since I had the bathroom to myself, I took a few minutes to give attention to my chapped lips and my hair. The water at Noelle's house seemed to make my hair fuller and fluffier. I tried to smooth the flyaway ends while looking in the black-framed mirror.

The mirror was old, with flecks of black in the surface, giving my reflection the same sort of aged and cracked image as many of the paintings we had seen up close yesterday. Those paintings were hundreds of years old. I wasn't quite half a century old.

I had a thought about the mystery of accepting all things temporal so I might fully welcome all things eternal. It was only half a thought. I wished I had some paper with me to write it down the way Noelle had taken notes for me earlier. I didn't fully know what the thought meant or if it even was meant for me.

I tilted my head and stared at my image as I fingered the ends of my hair. Would all that was temporal in me soon give way to all that was eternal? I knew the core of my essence, my soul, would go on forever because I had trusted Christ to be my Savior. He had made a way for me to come before my heavenly Father no longer covered in my sin but rather clothed in His righteousness.

When I died, I would be with Him forever in His home.

But before that became true…

I pulled all my hair back, away from my face. *What will I look like without any hair?*

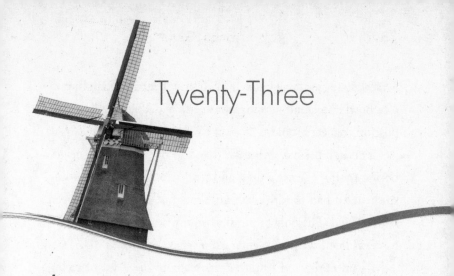

Twenty-Three

I pressed aside the thoughts of what I would look like if chemotherapy robbed me of my hair. Stepping out of the restaurant bathroom, I turned my attention to the light that came through the window at the end of the hall. The sunlight through the paned glass was accentuating the reds, golds, and blacks in the intricate pattern of a Persian runner on the floor.

Even though the stairs were to my left, I ventured to the right, curious to capture a closer view of the light streaming from the window.

The window was Vermeer's window.

Not the exact window that appeared in so many of his paintings, of course. We had learned that his house no longer was standing but that we were very close to the Delft neighborhood where he had lived and painted in his upstairs studio.

This window, with its misshapen glass and thick lead pieces separating the panes, could have been the same sort of window he painted by. The light came in at the same angle that I subconsciously had memorized after looking at the postcard of *The*

Milkmaid for so many years. If I had a pitcher of milk and a pottery bowl and stood just so, I was certain I could duplicate the pose of Vermeer's subject.

Through the hazy window, I took in the view of the neighboring rooftops. I felt a deep and tender longing in my settling spirit. If I'd had to formulate my thoughts, I would have been hard pressed. The only impression on my heart that I could capture was that I wanted to enter the eternal.

By no means did I think I was ready to die. I wasn't seeing visions of heaven or in any way welcoming the journey that would transport me from the temporal to the eternal. I wanted to stay here as long as I could, and nothing in me was at peace with the thought of undergoing some sort of treatment or suffering from a malady.

But in an oddly peaceful way, I was stirred by the thought of going to heaven. Just as I was stirred by the way the golden, luminous rays of the morning light broke through this distorted, decrepit window and left bits of fragmented glory all over the rug.

I returned to the table with my spirit in a wonderful tangle. I sipped my glass of freshly squeezed orange juice and told Noelle about the window, the light, and the hallway rug. As I tried to express how spiritual this venture to the Netherlands had been, her eyes never left mine.

"God feels very close right now for some reason."

Noelle leaned in and looked at me with an unblinking gaze. "I think so too. Now I am going to be Dutch and put a straightforward topic on the table. First I want you to tell me something."

"Okay."

"Summer, why did you come here?"

"To see you." The way my answer instantly rolled off my tongue surprised me.

"Why now?"

"It was a good time. It worked out."

She wasn't convinced and demonstrated that by not sitting back in her chair. She leaned forward even farther. "Now tell me the rest. Tell me the real reason."

I didn't answer.

"All right. If you won't tell me the true reason, then I will tell you what I think. I've thought about it, and I've come to two possible conclusions. Either you are contemplating having an affair—"

"No!"

"Then you won a lottery of some sort, and you're not telling me that you are now a millionaire."

"No. That's definitely not anywhere close to the truth."

"Then you will have to tell me the true reason, or else I will continue to come up with further guesses that will only embarrass you more."

"Can't we just leave things as they are?" I still was feeling a little glowy after my view of the light coming through the thick-paned window upstairs. I didn't want all the ethereal thoughts to be smashed by the cold harshness I would feel once my denial bubble was burst.

"I don't think it's a good idea to leave things unsaid. Not when you're only going to be in my corner of the world for such a short time. Besides, you forget how well I know you, Summer. I know how much you like things to be nice and orderly. Deciding on a whim to come here is not orderly. Something very large had to motivate you. Something larger than just the impulse that it was at long last time for us to meet face to face."

"Okay."

"I'm right, aren't I?"

"Yes." With a deep breath for courage, I began. "Here it is. I had an irregular mammogram last week. Actually, the word they used was 'abnormal.' I have to go back for a biopsy, and I decided I wanted to come here and meet you face to face before—"

"Oh, Summer." Noelle was out of her chair. Her arms were around me. She hugged my neck and held me tight.

I didn't cry. I think I was mad at myself for cracking out of my lovely denial shell. This was exactly the way I didn't want to be treated.

At the same time, something deep inside me said this was right. Noelle was the friend of my heart. It was right for me to tell her the truth.

Returning to her chair on the other side of the table, Noelle said with a sweet tenderness in her voice, "And you came here. Of all the things you could have done or places you could have gone, you came here to see me."

"Yes, I wanted to see you. And now you know why I decided so quickly. If things go for me as they did for my mother, I won't be able to travel much, so—"

"And if things don't go for you as they did for your mother,"—Noelle gave me a straightforward look—"then what? Have you thought about that?"

"If my case is more advanced, then I guess I make it a priority as soon as I get home to put my affairs in order." I hadn't expected Noelle to take such a blunt approach, especially right after hugging me and being so compassionate.

"No." She wagged her index finger back and forth as I had seen her do once or twice before when trying to make a point. "No. No. What if the diagnosis is not like your mother's? What if they take the biopsy and find nothing?"

I hadn't let my mind fully go in that direction.

"What will you do if all is well?"

"Keep living, I guess."

"Yes. You will. You will keep living as fully as you have been living this week. You will not become one of those women who stop too soon."

"What do you mean by that?"

"I mean, do not pick up a sack of fear and carry it with you everywhere, just waiting until the next test and diagnosis. Even if—especially if—this second test shows nothing. Do you know what I am saying? I have a friend here who has done this. She had one bad reading for her liver nine years ago. Since then all the tests have been fine. Clear. Even so, she decided it is only a matter of time before her liver fails, and she has made herself sick with the fear, even though she doesn't have a disease."

Noelle was speaking truth over me. It would be easy for me

to do the same thing as her friend had done, to stop living far too soon.

"Summer, how old was your mother when she passed away?"

"Seventy-nine."

"And how long ago was that? Ten years?"

"No, thirteen."

Noelle gave me a little rundown of how much the technology had improved in the past thirteen years and how so much could be done in the case of early detection.

I agreed, of course. She was right. I hadn't taken my thoughts down some of those roads yet, but even if the biopsy showed something serious, many steps could be taken to deal with the cancer.

My mother's breast cancer wasn't diagnosed until she was in stage four.

Maybe all would be well, as Noelle was saying.

Maybe.

"Look at Corrie ten Boom," Noelle said. "At fifty-three years old she thought she would die with her sister in the concentration camp. And for every practical reason, she should have. But God wasn't finished with her until she was ninety-one. Remember?"

I remembered.

Noelle gave me another wag of her finger. "You don't know what the results of the biopsy will be, but whatever they are, you can walk through any valley of the shadow of death and fear no evil. The Lord will be with you every step of the way."

"Yes, He will. I believe that." Of course it was easy to receive her pep talk on this side of the diagnosis. A week from now I didn't know how I would feel about her words.

The waitress arrived just then with our two large plates. The pancakes smelled wonderful.

Noelle reached across the table and covered my hand with hers. Together we bowed our heads and gave thanks for the pannenkoeken, for our friendship, and for the future, whatever it held for either of us.

After Noelle prayed, I prayed. I don't know what my words were, but I know that my feelings were different than they had been when I had tried to formulate prayers earlier that week. I felt humble, grateful, and appreciative of all of God's gracious provisions.

Cutting into the pancake, I took the first bite, accented by the warm baked apple topping, and chewed slowly.

At that moment God's blessings over my life seemed like the soft pink blossoms I had watched the morning breeze shake from the trees and toss in celebration over the two gliding swans in the canal. I can't say that, deep down, I still wasn't nervous and frightened about the future. But I felt a hint of longing for home—for heaven—after the events of the past few days.

That longing took the edge off my fears. This seemed to be the mystery I had thought about earlier when I was upstairs. Somehow it coincided with the thoughts I'd had in the cheese shop—the sacredness of the everyday.

I reached in my purse and pulled out the papers that Noelle had written earlier. At the bottom of her writing, I scribbled my incomplete thoughts:

The sacredness of the everyday. The mystery of accepting all things temporal so that I might fully welcome all things eternal. The longing for home is ultimately the longing for heaven.

"What are you writing?"

"I don't know."

"Well, when you do, send me a copy."

"Always." I smiled at my pen pal.

"We hold each other's lifetime of collected thoughts, don't we?"

"Maybe we should switch sometime. I'll send you all your letters, and you send me all mine."

"I like that idea," Noelle said. "That's what we can give each other for our birthdays this year. Did I tell you we have a tradition here on birthdays? When it is someone's birthday, everyone congratulates their family."

"Yes, the first night I was here Jelle told me about that tradition."

"That's right. Well, on my birthday my husband's family all come by or call him to say congratulations. I always tell Jelle they are congratulating him for finding such a wonderful woman."

"Then on Jelle's birthday do they congratulate you?"

"Yes. Of course. I tell them they must be congratulating me for living with such a difficult man for so long. That always makes his family roll their eyes. Jelle is the easiest one in their family to get along with. He's wonderful, as you might have noticed."

"Yes, I did notice. Congratulations, even though it isn't your birthday or Jelle's birthday. Congratulations for making a fine choice of a husband."

Noelle looked down at her hands and seemed to be reflecting on something more profound than my last comment.

"You know," she said without looking up, "I didn't realize it until just now, but I think I have been waiting my whole married life to hear those words. Not from you, but from my dad. I always wanted him to change his mind about me and Jelle and come back to me and say, 'Congratulations. You married a fine man. You made something good of your life.'"

She looked up, her eyes glistening. "But since I will probably never hear those words from him, I'm just as happy to take them from you. Thank you, Summer."

With our hearts full of sisterly affirmations and our bellies full of pannenkoeken, we left the restaurant and strolled through some of the neighboring shops. One of them was the shop Noelle had mentioned earlier where we could watch the Delft tiles being painted.

We stood for a long while with our hands behind our backs, appreciating the intricate detail work of the pottery painters as they carried on the centuries-old craft of putting their thin, blue paint–laden brushes to a blank plate, tile, or vase and turning it into a signature piece of art.

What followed was a meander through a bookstore and then a long stay at a small antique store. The proprietor lived above the showroom and made several trips up and down the stairs while Noelle and I took our time going through the hundreds of Delft tiles he had in boxes lined up on the floor. Each tile was different. Some of them looked similar until we held the two side by side to compare.

Most of the tiles were chipped. Many were broken in at least one place. A few had been repaired with glue that had turned brown over the years along the break line.

All the tiles, he claimed, were at least a hundred and fifty years old. Many of them he guaranteed to be three hundred years old. The prices varied, depending on age.

"He says his son is a renovator. He takes down parts of the old houses here in Delft and restores them."

"Like the restaurant we were just at."

"Yes. He probably did that restoration. He pulls down the tiles, and his father sells them. They know the year of the house and the year of the tiles by the city documents they have to sign before the work begins. You can see how he has them carefully organized. That's why he said we may look all we want, but he will keep an eye over us to make sure we put everything back as it should be. Although here, on the back of each tile, he has written in pencil the year of the house."

I admit I've enjoyed an occasional yard sale or rummage sale at the church. But I never had enjoyed a treasure hunt as much as I enjoyed going through those hundreds of tiles with Noelle.

I think we found so much glee in the task because both of us had experienced a sort of soul bath there in Delft. We were like a couple of best friends fresh from a plunge in the lake at junior high summer camp, and now we were given a project to work on as a team. Just Noelle-o Mell-o and me.

Our objective was to find two tiles that went together or in some way complemented each other. Our plan was for each of us to take our tile and put it in a place of prominence in our kitchen. Whenever we looked at our matching/complementing tiles, we would remember this day, and we would pray for each other.

"This is the absolute best sort of souvenir." I took off my coat in the warm, cramped space and sat cross-legged on the floor next to Noelle.

The shop owner was eager to help us in our quest. He had a "private reserve" of his favorites tucked away upstairs and was willing to let us purchase a couple of the special tiles.

I didn't know if that was a ploy to garner more money from us since he could tell we were intent on not leaving his shop until a significant purchase had been made. He could have been sincere in his eagerness to share. Although, the eager salesman had a half-dozen boxes of the private reserves, so I didn't feel too bad about robbing him of his private bounty.

After a while the windmills, church spires, and little Dutch girls herding geese with sticks began to look the same. Blue lines. Lots of blue lines. I also was forgetting about the specific directions Noelle had given me on what to look for in the corner of the tiles.

"Did you say the more valuable ones are the ones with the squiggles in the corner or the ones with just a thin line?"

She handed over her sample tile. "Like this. These are apparently more valuable because they were made at the most renowned kiln here in Delft. This is the top of the line. Although at this point we just need to make a decision, Summer."

The owner, who had been watching closely, picked up on my name. "Summer?"

"Yes?"

"Zomer?" he repeated it in Dutch and then pointed to Noelle and said her name.

I had no idea what he was getting at, but Noelle did. Her expression brightened, and she laughed.

"What? I missed that entirely."

"Apparently both of us did."

"What?"

"I never saw this before." She looked incredulous. "I can't believe I never saw this before."

"You're killing me here! What didn't you ever see before?"

"You're Summer, and I'm Noelle."

"Yes? And?"

"You and I are opposite seasons. Summer." She pointed at me. "And winter or Christmas or Noel."

"Wow, I never thought of that either."

"Opposites attract, right?" Noelle said. "No wonder we have been so good for each other all these years."

"I know just the tiles for us. I had one of them in my hand a few seconds ago."

With some careful rearranging of stacks, I pulled out a tile that was only missing about a quarter of an inch of the top left corner. The scene was of a tree with widespread branches. Under the tree was the figure of a young girl reaching up to pick fruit and place it in her basket. The three intact corners bore the right kind of squiggle to put the tile into the Delft pottery category. That part was important to both of us.

"And the other one is in this box. Help me look for it. It's a winter scene with an ice skater on a frozen canal with a windmill in the background."

"I get where you're going with this. A summer scene and a winter scene. Very clever, Summer Breeze."

"Glad you like it, Noelle-o Mell-o."

"Quite right."

The tiles were expensive. Most treasures are. The shop owner seemed as delighted with the results of our hunt as we were. He said he was giving us a discount because we were buying the two, but who knows if it was actually twice the price and he was trying to make it a victorious experience for us. It didn't matter.

With our winter and summer tiles safely wrapped and tucked into our shoulder bags, we went in search of chocolate. How else would we celebrate such a successful treasure hunt?

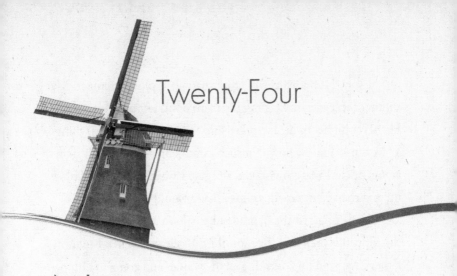

Twenty-Four

Noelle pulled out a chair at the tiny corner table inside a book shop that was not far from the antique store where we found our treasured tiles. I waited, looking out the window at the mix of afternoon shoppers on the narrow cobblestone street.

She returned with two cups of rich, dark, hot Dutch chocolate. As we were sitting in that cozy corner sipping the lovely chocolate, I suddenly felt very Dutch and wanted to open a difficult topic. I looked at Noelle the way she had looked at me while we were at the pancake house.

"What?" she asked, obviously aware that my gaze had turned intense and questioning.

"Noelle, how did your relationship with your father get so broken?"

She moved her unused napkin to the side and placed her cup on the table, looking down. "You have learned a lot in your short visit, haven't you? Put the question right out there."

I considered retracting my question, but for some reason this felt right. All of it.

"Okay, I'll tell you. My father had an explosive temper. My mother succeeded in keeping the truth of his temper from others. He never hit her or us. He yelled and threatened and threw things a few times. I know now that such treatment is emotionally damaging, but as I was growing up, all I knew was that he would blow up and then calm down, and we never would talk about it."

Noelle fingered the handle of her spoon and looked down as she flipped it back and forth on the tablecloth. "When I told my father I was thinking of taking all my savings and going to Europe, he lost it. I don't know why his reaction was so intense, but he said that if I dared leave the house and go all the way to Europe, I should never come back home."

"Why?"

"I think he was afraid. That's all I can figure out. He was afraid something would happen to me. He never said that, and I didn't understand that sort of parental concern. All I knew was that he was enraged for days, and his anger didn't let up. He hollered and threatened a lot. I was afraid he would hit me. And I wondered if he did hit me, would he stop? My only course seemed to be to get out from under his roof to avoid his rage.

"The day I left I thought he might calm down and simply accept my choice. But he was even angrier that I was exerting such independence from him. He struck me across the face, called me a vile name, and yelled, 'Get out of my sight!' Then he turned his back on me and punched a hole through the wall by the front door. I grabbed my luggage and ran down the front steps with blood dripping from my mouth. I never looked back."

"Noelle, how awful!"

"I know. It was. I found a new life here with Jelle and his family, and I just went on. My parents never came to see me. My mom sent some beautiful gifts for our wedding and signed the card from both of them, but I knew my dad wasn't part of the gift giving or the celebrating. My father never got over my leaving, and I believe he used his violent behavior to keep my mother from coming to see me, even when the girls were born."

We sat quietly in the somberness of her story.

"I lost so much because of him. I thought it was too late for anything to change, but now I wonder if there might be a chance."

"It's not too late," I said firmly. "To reconcile with your father, I mean."

"I know. I'm getting there." With half a grin she added, "Thanks to you and your visit."

"What do you mean?"

"None of these issues or feelings had surfaced for a long time. You show up, and everything that really matters is suddenly at the forefront. The past and the present began to mingle the moment you arrived." She reached across the table and squeezed my hand. "You probably thought God brought you here because you needed this time to think about the future. Maybe He also brought you here because I needed to think about the past."

I nodded and sipped my chocolate. "We both needed this time together."

"Just like we have both needed each other since the beginning." Noelle traced the rim of her cup with her finger. "Wouldn't our teachers be surprised to know what they started with their simple pen pal assignment?"

I drained the last of my delicious drink and made a successful attempt at communicating my delight. With the palm of my open hand fluffing up my hair, I said, "Lekker!"

Noelle beamed at my accomplishment.

"I think it's your turn now."

"My turn for what? I already speak English."

"No, it's your turn to come see me. Soon. Very soon."

She tilted her head. "Maybe."

"No maybes. Only yesses. You and Jelle need to come visit us."

We lingered a bit longer before deciding that Delft probably had a few more shops we should explore.

The first was a small but amazing flower market. We bought tulips by the bunches, lifting them right out of the white buckets and letting them drip water all over our feet. I bought three bunches of tulips, and Noelle bought two. We looked like beauty pageant queens, cradling our lovely bouquets on the way to the next hot-spot shop Noelle insisted we go to.

I saw the store she was eager to visit before we were halfway there. The rack of colorfully painted wares on the outside was the hint.

"You're going to make me buy a pair of wooden shoes, aren't you?"

"Quite right."

I was a willing customer, and she was a persistent assistant. For every pair she showed me, I bit my lower lip and scrunched up my nose. Then she would return with two more just as color-fully painted and just as clunky.

I knew she wouldn't give up. And truthfully, I didn't want her to. When she pointed at the bright yellow pair with the red tulips painted on the side, I knew those were the ones.

"Just like our boat," she said.

I tried them on and laughed at how large my feet looked in the bright yellow clogs. "I feel as if each of these is a little boat in and of itself. I could go water-skiing with these, and they would keep me afloat."

"Those are the pair then?" Noelle asked.

"Yes, these are the winners."

"Give them to me, and I'll pay for them. They are my gift to you."

I stuck my chin out with mock defiance. "And what if I want to wear them out of the shop?"

Noelle gave me a second look. "You wouldn't really, would you?"

"Why not?" I confided in her that my blister was killing me in spite of the plaster I had applied. The wooden shoes didn't hit my sore heel at all. I would look ridiculous, true. But my feet would be much happier than they'd been all day in my irritating shoes.

She warned me that I would be a spectacle and then walked away to pay for the wooden shoes. I left them on my feet and reached for the bountiful combined bouquet of tulips. If I was going to be a spectacle, I might as well be a colorful spectacle.

We headed for the next store, and I said, "Even though I walk through the streets of Delft in wooden shoes, I will fear no mocking from the bystanders."

"You really have worked out just about every possible paraphrase on that psalm, haven't you?"

"I have one more version I've been working on in the back of my mind. Do you still have that little notebook in your purse?"

"Yes. Do you want me to take dictation again?"

"No, I want to borrow it on our drive home."

After another hour of shopping, I managed to find souvenirs for everyone on my list. I received a steady stream of stares at my flowers and shoes along with a variety of comments in a variety of languages. Noelle understood some of them and assured me that not all my critics were favorable toward my best-foot-forward choice of attire.

I didn't care. Not really. So much of what mattered to me on this trip had been those things that happened on the inside. The outward didn't concern me as much as it had before.

We trotted back to Noelle's secret parking spot, and I couldn't wait to slip out of the jolly wooden shoes. My feet now had blisters in new places.

"You wanted this?" Noelle held out the notepad.

"Oh, right. I almost forgot."

While she drove, I wiggled my toes and composed. My paraphrase was complete before we arrived home. "Are you ready for this?"

"Probably not, but I have a feeling that won't stop you from reading it to me."

I cleared my throat and read the masterpiece scribbled on the notepad:

The Lord is my shepherd; I shall not freak out.
He makes me lie down under scanning machines,
He leads me to trustworthy doctors,
He restores my deductible.
Even though I walk through the valley of the shadow of death
(And keep on walking and don't get stuck or sit down and
*   have a hissy fit),*
I will fear no evil,
For You are with me.
Your new creation health renewal plan
And perfect timing, they comfort me.
You prepare an organic diet before me
In the presence of my injections.
You anoint my bald head with oil
When my bra cup no longer overflows.
Surely goodness and mercy shall follow me all the days of my life,
And eventually I will come live in Your house, forever!

Noelle's first response was to laugh, but with her airy giggle came a stream of tears. I cried too. Good tears. Tears that cleansed and revived and took their time to roll down because each one of them meant to make its journey deliberate.

Jelle was home when we arrived and tucked little Bluebell into her compact parking spot in front of the house. He said he wanted to take us out to dinner, if we were interested, which we were.

Our reservations were for eight o'clock. I headed upstairs to the pleasant guest room and went to work packing my bags. We had to leave the house at six in the morning to reach the airport in time for my flight home.

This had been one of the fastest weeks of my life. Fastest and fullest.

I went to the devotional book beside the bed and gave it a loving pat. When we had arrived at her house, Noelle had told me to keep her purse-sized notebook. She said it had proved that day that it much preferred holding my thoughts than holding her shopping lists.

With the gracious little gift open in my hand, I flipped through the devotional book, looking for the entry that had brought me such comfort my first morning in this room. When I located the verses in 2 Corinthians 4, I copied them in Noelle's notepad: "So we're not giving up. How could we! Even though on the outside it often looks like things are falling apart on us, on the inside, where God is making new life, not a day goes by without his unfolding grace.... The things we see now are here today, gone tomorrow. But the things we can't see now will last forever."

The passage had such a different meaning to me now than it had a few days ago. Noelle had urged me at lunch not to give in to fear and start shutting down my life. Corrie ten Boom thought she was going to die when she was in midlife, and yet she went on to travel the world for the next three-plus decades.

My eyes fixed on the phrase "unfolding grace." I liked that phrase so much. I knew it would always remind me of the tulips we visited my first day here. All those millions of brilliant blooms would be here today and gone tomorrow. But their bulbs, the essential core of everything they were, would go on and be sent around the world.

I couldn't wait to tell Wayne everything I had discovered on this trip. I was ready to go home. Ready to face whatever came next.

Noelle tapped on the guest room door. "Summer Breeze?"

"Yes?"

"Wooden shoe like to come join us for dinner?" The lightness in her voice made it clear that she was impressed with her own play on words.

In my deepest, mellowest voice I replied, "Quite right."

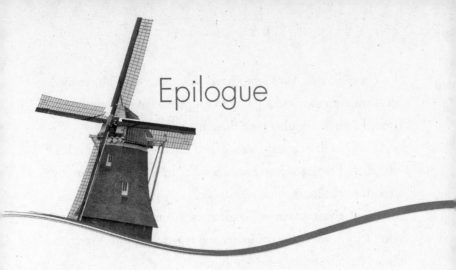

Epilogue

The call came at 4:15 on Thursday afternoon, five days after I had returned from the Netherlands.

"Normal" was the word the medical assistant used.

"Normal?"

"Yes, normal."

I fumbled to ask the "why was it different last time" question instead of the "what's next" question I had prepared myself to ask.

"Given your family medical history, it appears that your doctor wanted to have a closer look to be extra careful. He saw something in the mammogram and wanted to be sure everything was okay. Apparently you have dense breasts."

I hung up and looked down at my chest. "Don't listen to her. You two aren't that dense. A bit droopy maybe, but all of us need a little more support as we get older."

I dialed Wayne's number at work and repeated the good news. He was choked up and told me four times how glad he was. Then he said he wanted to take me out to dinner. Chinese.

I realized that, for my husband, going out for Chinese food was similar to the Dutch going to eat pannenkoeken when they needed a place to gather their thoughts.

And Noelle was right about the Dutch word for pancakes. The more I repeated it to our kids while telling them about my adventure, the more fun it was to say.

After agreeing to meet Wayne at the Chinese restaurant in an hour, I sat down at the computer and typed the word *Normal* in the subject line of my e-mail to Noelle.

"Normal," I said aloud again. "Normal."

It amazed me how much life could happen between the words *abnormal* and *normal.* Those sixteen days of unfolding grace had changed my heart and my life.

I realized that, genetically, nothing had changed. Cancer could well be the vehicle that one day would take my earthly body on the inevitable float down the canal to eternity.

But not this day.

This day was for living. For fully living without giving way to fear.

Wayne and I dreamed big over our pot stickers and Kung Pao chicken. He told me he'd always wanted to go to Argentina since his grandmother was born there. Perhaps, he said, we could put away some money and travel there in a year or so.

I was all for it.

I woke the next morning at 3:15. Lingering jet lag, it seems, was one of the souvenirs I had brought home with me. After padding downstairs, just as I had done two weeks earlier when I was awaiting Noelle's formal invitation to visit her, I sat in front of the computer's glowing screen.

With a few clicks of the mouse, I waited for my e-mail file to open.

There it was. Noelle's response to my "Normal" pronouncement from the previous afternoon. I tried to picture where she was at the moment, which sweater she was wearing, and whether she had a new bouquet of tulips adorning her dining room table.

The last line of her e-mail was the best. After offering her cheers for the diagnosis, she wrote, "Jelle and I have decided to take you up on your offer. We would like to come the first week of June to see you and your family for five days before flying on to Wyoming. We're going to see my father."

With happy tears filling my eyes, I typed back as quickly as I could. The subject line of my e-mail contained one simple, perfect, life-changing word: "Come!"

Reader's Guide

1. Summer's response to the news of an abnormal mammogram was to bake cookies and plan a trip to Holland. Have you ever received a scary medical report? If so, what was your response? If not, how do you imagine you would respond?

2. Summer and Noelle maintained a long-distance friendship for much of their lives. When the opportunity to meet in person presented itself, Summer realized there was so much she didn't know about Noelle (such as her gait when she walks and whether or not she wears perfume). If you imagine your first meeting with God upon your arrival in heaven, which of His characteristics do you wonder about?

3. Upon meeting Noelle's husband, Summer was mortified that she mispronounced his name. Sometimes we find ourselves in awkward situations due to cultural or language differences. Share a time when you felt embarrassed at your own cultural naiveté. What helped you through the uncomfortable feelings?

4. After a candlelit dinner with Noelle and Jelle, Summer felt honored by the leisurely time they had spent

together. Think of a time when you felt honored by a friend or a family member. In what ways did that person show honor? What impact did that event have on your relationship?

5.   In the tulip fields Summer felt like a child experiencing one of the simple wonders of the world for the first time. Describe an occasion when you paused to take in the beauty of God's creation. What did you see or hear? What wonder did it stir in you?

6.   As Summer awkwardly milked the cow at the dairy farm, Noelle admonished her with these words: "The next time you face something new that you think you don't want to do, remember this moment, Summer. Remember this feeling. You can do all things through Christ, who strengthens you." Describe a time when you had to rely on Christ to strengthen you in order to do something outside your comfort zone. How did you feel? What did you learn about yourself in the process?

7.   Summer was perplexed at her own quick judgment when Noelle told her that Zahida was a Christian. Have you ever assumed something about another person only to learn that the opposite was true? Was fear or prejudice at the root of it? How might you respond today if you were to encounter a similar situation?

8. During their visit to Corrie ten Boom's home, Summer mentioned having a "tender flash." She described it as "one of those heartwarming moments when heaven suddenly seems real. What follows is an unexpected calm, accompanied by a feeling of anticipation, or maybe it would be more accurate to call it a longing for home, as in heaven." What does the idea of a "tender flash" bring to mind for you? When have you felt a longing for heaven?

9. During their friendship, Noelle and Summer occasionally experienced long stretches—sometimes months—of silence. Yet they were good at picking up wherever they had left off and taking their friendship on from there. Share about a Sisterchick friendship of your own that maintains a strong bond even over time or distance. What are the ingredients that keep that relationship thriving?

10. As Summer and Noelle floated down the canal in the wooden-shoe boat, Summer's out-of-character response was to laugh and to wave at the people along the water's edge. Sometimes life presents circumstances that are beyond our control. Do you tend to get serious in such a situation, or do you allow yourself to "go with the flow," so to speak? How might a little humor help you through something beyond your control?

11. At the museum in Amsterdam, Noelle and Summer realized that Noelle's choice to move to Holland had changed the course of both of their lives. They agreed that they liked the way things had turned out. What is one choice you made in younger years that took you on a particular path? How would your life be different had you chosen a different option? In what ways can you see God's hand in the direction you took?

12. Just as tulips reminded Summer and Noelle of God's unfolding grace, their Sisterchick friendship unfolded into full bloom as each woman shared the deepest cares of her heart. With whom do you share your deepest cares? How does that person help you experience God's unfolding grace?

Bonus Material for

*Sisterchicks
in Wooden
Shoes!*

Hello, dear Sisterchick!

One of my greatest delights in writing the Sisterchick novels has
been the journeys I've taken around the world while researching
the location of each book. (I know, what a writer's dream!) If I
could take you with me on these adventures, oh, what a time we
would have! Since that's not possible, I thought you might enjoy
seeing a few snapshots and hearing a few of the stories behind the
story for *Sisterchicks in Wooden Shoes!*

VISITING MY SOUL SISTERCHICK, ANNE

I met Anne at the Frankfurt International Book Fair fourteen years
ago. (We look so young!) We found out both of us were novelists,
and from there the similarities kept growing. Our fast-formed

friendship has taken us many places around the world for speaking and writing opportunities. Anne has lived in the Netherlands for more than twenty-five years, so whenever we see each other, it's because one or both of us have "jumped across the puddle."

Robin and Anne in the early years

VISITING ANNE IN HOLLAND

When I turned fifty, my wonderful husband gave me a heartfelt gift to celebrate the fact that it had been ten years since I'd had a series of surgeries, including one where a malignant growth was removed. His gift was a plane ticket to the Netherlands so I could visit Anne in her home. No writing or speaking events were planned for this visit. Just Sisterchick time. However, being an incurable storyteller, I confess that I came home with a little story in the back of my mind. It was a story about a couple of Sisterchicks in wooden shoes who didn't let fear make all the decisions for them.

Anne in Delft as she showed me the market square

Photo by Robin Gunn

UPSTAIRS AT THE PANNENKOEKENHUIS IN DELFT

At lunchtime during our day in Delft, Anne and I found a restaurant that served the much-advertised pannenkoeken. When I went upstairs to use the rest room, my experience was very close to what Summer experienced in the story. The window resembled the

The pancake restaurant in Delft with the amazing Vermeer-like window

Photo by Anne de Graaf

windows that appeared in Vermeer's paintings, and the view seemed as if it hadn't changed in hundreds of years. I grabbed the vase of tulips that adorned a corner table at the top of the stairs and grinned broadly for the shot. We found out later that Vermeer's original house had been torn down years ago, but it had been located very close to the house that had been turned into a restaurant. With their being so similar, it was easy to imagine Vermeer sitting in such light by such a window while painting *The Girl with the Pearl Earring.*

ANTIQUE STORE

I loved this little antique and curiosity shop. I bought two genuine Delft tiles here: one for my mom and one for my sister. Did you notice the wooden shoes in the right bottom corner? Yellow even. More than once I have regretted not buying a pair of authentic wooden shoes while I was there. Why? I don't know. Just because. That's why Noelle had to persuade Summer to pick out a pair of wooden shoes.

Photo by Anne de Graaf

Antique shop in Delft

Wooden Shoe Like to Go for a Ride?

The characters in the Sisterchicks novels have chances to do the things I only wish I'd done when I was visiting the countries featured in each book. Such as float down a canal in Amsterdam in a wooden-shoe boat. I floated in a traditional tour boat, but when I saw this little honey of a boat, I thought, *Now* that *would be the way to go!* My imagination took it from there.

The yellow wooden-shoe boat in Amsterdam

The New Church in Delft (1358!)

In the same way that Summer was stunned when she entered the New Church in Delft and found it to be stark, I was surprised when Anne took me there. Such grandeur on the outside but so stripped down and solemn on the inside. I missed the softness that art and beauty bring to an environment. At the same time, the lack of lots of décor allowed for a simple, clarifying time of reflection, which is what happened with Noelle in the story.

Photo by Robin Jones Gunn

Delft church

Stop and Smell the Tulips!

It's all about the tulips! Even though I've visited the Netherlands on several occasions, I've not yet visited at the height of tulip season. However, my original Sisterchick, Donna, and I found a field alive with blooming glories a short drive south of where we live near Portland, Oregon. Oh, the bliss of bobbing along in a field of such beauty!

Me, taking time to tickle the tulips in Oregon

Photo by Donna Hendrix

Little Dutch Girl

Yes, this is about as silly as any author would want to appear while in the midst of all-important research for a book. I needed to get in touch with my inner Dutch woman. Every time I look at this picture, it makes me laugh. Maybe it will bring a giggle to you as well.

Photo by Donna Hendrix

Me as a little Dutch girl

A FEW TIPS ON SOME REAL DUTCH TREATS

- Getting around: Since the Netherlands is a small country and the rail system is wonderfully efficient, you'll have no trouble seeing the countryside from the train window. As a bonus, you won't have to hunt for parking when you arrive at your destination. However, for getting around in any of the larger cities, bikes really are the way to go. And go, and go, and go.

- Tulip season: For half a century several amazing gardens, such as the Keukenhof, have been showing off their tulips each spring to visitors from all over the world. The Web site http://us.holland.com gives all the details on where to go and when.

-◐ Dutch chocolate: There really is a difference. Dutch chocolate is less acidic and has a milder flavor. I think it has a natural creaminess that allows the sipping chocolate to take its sweet time sliding down the throat. The Dutch chocolate maker who developed this process also created a method for removing fat from cacao beans. Therefore, I like to pretend that Dutch chocolate has no fat. Would you like to pretend with me?

-◐ The Hiding Place: When I was in college, I had the delight of meeting Tante Corrie and hearing her speak a number of times. Even if you don't have the privilege of visiting the Netherlands, I hope you'll visit www .corrietenboom.com or gather your family and watch the movie *The Hiding Place.* I can't wait to see Corrie again in heaven!

Please come visit my Web site and sign up to receive the Robin's Nest newsletter. I'd love to keep in touch and update you on new releases as well as let you know about drawings for free books and book signings in your area.

www.robingunn.com

www.sisterchicks.com